Kinky Friedman lives in a little green trailer in a valley deep in the heart of Texas. There are about ten million imaginary horses in the valley and quite often they gallop around Kinky's trailer, encircling the author in a terrible, ever-tightening carousel of death. Even as the hooves are pounding around him in the darkest night, one can hear, almost in counterpoint, the frail, consumptive, ascetic novelist tip-tip-tapping away on the last typewriter in Texas. In such fashion he has turned out ten novels including *Roadkill*, *The Love Song of J. Edgar Hoover*, *God Bless John Wayne*, *Armadillos & Old Lace* and *Elvis, Jesus & Coca-Cola*. Two cats, Dr Scat and Lady Argyle, a pet armadillo called Dilly, and a small black dog named Mr Magoo can some-times be found sleeping with Kinky in his narrow, monastic, Father Damien-like bed.

When the Cat's Away
KINKY FRIEDMAN

*For the Cat
with no name!*

*Love,
Kinky*

ff
faber and faber
LONDON · BOSTON

18/8/99

First published in the United States of America in 1988
by William Morrow and Company, Inc., New York
First published in Great Britain in 1992 in
The Kinky Friedman Crime Club
This UK paperback edition published in 1998
by Faber and Faber Limited
3 Queen Square, London WC1N 3AU

Phototypeset by Intype London Ltd
Printed and bound in Great Britain by
Mackays of Chatham PLC, Chatham, Kent

A CIP record for this book is
available from the British Library

ISBN 0-571-19413-3

2 4 6 8 10 9 7 5 3 1

For Kacey Cohen,
The angel on my shoulder

One magic midnight show
She taught you how it feels
Once, oh so long ago
When rock 'n' roll was real

Acknowledgments

The author would like to thank the following people for their help: Tom Friedman, Earl Buckelew, Marcie Friedman, and Larry 'Ratso' Sloman; Esther 'Lobster' Newberg at ICM; James Landis, Jane Meara, and Lori Ames at Beech Tree Books; and Steve Rambam, technical adviser. The author would also like to express his thanks to the following officials of the Garden Cat Club: Vicky Markstein, Peter Markstein and Elinor Silverman.

When the Cat's Away

Winnie Katz's lesbian dance class was like God. Mankind never saw it, but you always knew it was there.

Of course Moses had seen God. In the form of a burning bush, interestingly enough. Then he took two tablets and went to bed.

There are people who have seen God since, but we have a place for them. It is called Bellevue and the area around it, for a twenty-block radius, is regarded as having one of the highest violent-crime rates in the city. That's because it's impossible to tell who's insane in New York.

Every seven minutes they let a perfectly normal-looking guy out of Bellevue. He walks a block or two, buys a pretzel on the street, asks somebody what time it is, then has a flashback to the Peloponnesian War. He takes out a Swiss Army knife and cuts some Korean woman's head off. Uses the wrong blade. The one you're supposed to cut nose hairs with. Of course, it isn't his fault.

Not everybody's had the opportunity to be in the Swiss Army.

I listened to the rhythmic thuddings in the loft above me. I wondered what the hell was really going on up there. If somebody's wayward daughter from Coeur d'Alene, Idaho, was being broken down like a double-barreled shotgun, it'd be a hell of a lot of early ballroom lessons gone to waste. On the other hand, what did I know about modern dance?

It was a chilly evening in late January and I was sitting at my desk just sort of waiting for something besides my New Year's resolutions to kick in. If you're patient and you wait long enough, something will usually happen and it'll usually be something you don't like. I poured a generous slug of Jameson Irish whiskey into the old bull's horn that I sometimes used as a shotglass. I killed the shot.

Like my pal McGovern always says: gets rid of the toothpaste taste.

I was dreaming the unisexual dreams of the everyday houseperson, when the phones rang. There are two red telephones in my loft, both connected to the same line, at stage left and stage right of my desk. When you're sitting at the desk they ring simultaneously on either side of what you're pleased to call your brain. While this may upgrade the significance of any incoming wounded you're likely to receive, it can also make you want to jump into your boots and slide down the pole.

I woke with a start, which was a good thing. Daydreaming while smoking cigars can be a fire hazard. It can be as dangerous as drugs and booze unless you know what you're doing. If you know what you're doing, it can be as safe as walking down the street. Long as you're not daydreaming within a twenty-block radius of Bellevue.

2

I watched the phones ring for a while. I'd been dreaming about a girl in a peach-colored dress. Another couple of rings wasn't going to hurt anybody. I took a leisurely puff on the cigar and picked up the blower on the left.

'Spit it,' I said.

A woman was sobbing on the other end of the line. I tried to identify her by her sob but I couldn't. Maybe it was a wrong number.

Finally, the voice collected itself somewhat and said, 'Kinky. Kinky. This . . . this is Jane Meara.' Jane Meara was

4

a friend of mine, a pretty, perky, intelligent girl and one of the authors of the book *Growing Up Catholic*. At the moment it didn't sound like she'd grown up at all.

Grieving women are not my long suit. I have found, however, that a direct, almost gruff demeanor is usually quite effective. Anyway, it was all I had in stock.

'Jane,' I said, 'pull yourself together. What the hell's the matter? Your guppies die?'

This, apparently, broke the dam. A heartfelt wail was now coming down the line. I put the blower down on the desk. I puffed several times rapidly on my cigar. When I picked up again it was just in time to hear Jane saying, 'I wish, I wish my guppies *had* died.'

'C'mon, Jane,' I said, 'what is it? You're cuttin' into my cocktail hour.'

I could hear her shoulders stiffen. She sniffled a few more times. Then she said, 'My cat's disappeared.'

'Relax, Jane,' I said. 'We'll get it back. What's the cat's name?'

'Rocky.'

'What's he look like?'

'It's a she.'

'Fine.'

I got the pertinent details from Jane. Rocky was yellow and white with four white paws. According to Jane she 'looked like she was wearing sweat socks.' Rocky'd disappeared – vanished into thin air – right in the middle of a cat show in Madison Square Garden. Jane had stepped away for just a moment and when she'd returned the cage was empty and the cat was gone.

I pressed Jane for a little more information, made some reassuring noises, and gave her my word I'd hop right on it.

I hung up, walked over to the kitchen window, and

watched the gloom settle over the city. Monday night and it looked like it.

The cat show, according to Jane, would be purring along all week and would be closing each night at nine. It was now nudging seven o'clock. I'd have to work fairly fast.

If the cat was still in the Garden, there was always a chance. She might wind up on the wrong end of a hockey stick, but there was a chance.

If Rocky'd gotten out of the Garden and into the street, getting her back would be tough.

Almost as tough as getting back a girl in a peach-colored dress.

3

Finding lost cats is not the most romantic, macho experience a country-singer-turned-amateur-detective might get into. But there was something rather poignant about the hopelessness of Jane Meara's situation that I couldn't bend my conscience quite enough to ignore.

I puffed on my cigar and reflected that I'd never much liked cats myself. Until one winter night about eight years ago in an alley in Chinatown when I'd met the first pussy that ever swept me off my feet.

Now I have a cat. Well, that's not quite accurate. A cat and I have each other. We inhabit a large, drafty loft on the fourth floor of a converted warehouse at 199B Vandam, New York City.

In the summer the loft is hotter than Equatorial West Topsyland. In the winter it's so cold you have to jump-start your electric toothbrush. The landlord has promised to do something about it. The cat and I live in hope.

Cats, country music, and cigars have become the three spiritual linchpins of my life. Actually, I have a few other

6

spiritual linchpins and they also begin with a *c*, but we won't go into that now.

If I was going to find Jane's cat, I'd better get cracking.

I called Ratso, a friend of mine who, over the past few years, had accompanied me in solving several rather ugly murder cases in the Village. Ratso was loud, garish, and fiscally tight as a tick, but he was also warm, loyal, and blessed with an ingenuous spirit. He was as worthy a modern-day Dr Watson as I was ever likely to find. Good help is hard to get these days.

Ratso was not home so I tried him at the office. He was the editor of the *National Lampoon*. Maybe he was working late, I thought. He answered the phone himself.

'Leprosarium for Unwed Mothers,' he said.

'Ratso,' I said, 'it's Kinky. I need your help. I'm looking for a lost cat. It got away at the cat show down at the Garden.'

My words were greeted by laughter and hoots of derision. It became quickly apparent to me that Ratso had put me on the speaker phone. I could hear Mike Simmons, the other editor of the magazine, shout, 'If you find that pussy, give me a call.' There was more laughter. I was beginning to run out of charm.

'Ratso,' I said, 'either you're coming or you're not.'

Simmons shouted again, 'That's what she told him last night.' That one seemed to crack up the whole office.

'Listen, Kinkster,' said Ratso, 'you and I've got better things to do than run around New York looking for a lost fucking cat. You're a hero, Kinkster.' I winced slightly and took a puff on the cigar.

Ratso continued, 'You solved the Worthington case. You got McGovern off the hook. Remember?'

''Fraid so,' I said.

'You saved the girl at the bank from the mugger.'

7

'Anybody could've.'

'But anybody *didn't* – you did. That's why you're *some-body*. You're hot. You're happening! You can pick and choose, baby.'

'Look,' I said, 'it's just something I've gotten myself into. I'll go down there alone.'

There was a moment of silence on the line. Then Ratso said, 'All right, I'll meet you at the Garden. Window eleven. Fifteen minutes.'

'Make it ten,' I said. 'We take any longer, this cat's gonna be out at LaGuardia asking for an aisle seat in the non-smoking section.'

As I hung up I heard Ratso mutter something to himself. It sounded very much like 'Fucking cat.'

I put on my hat and my old hunting vest and took three cigars for the road. I put them in the little stitched pockets of the vest where some Americans keep their shotgun shells.

'You see,' I said to my own cat as I left for the Garden, 'he's not such a terrible Watson after all.'

4

Ratso was waiting for me at window 11. He looked like an amiable pimp. He wore a coonskin cap minus the tail, fuchsia slacks, and red flea-market shoes that, as I often pointed out to him, had once belonged to a dead man. To round it off, he wore a blue sweatshirt that said NATIONAL LAMPOON COHABITATION TEAM.

'Nice outfit,' I said. 'You look like the Don Juan of all ticket scalpers.'

'Thanks,' he said. 'Wardrobe by Hadassah Thrift Shop.'

We walked down the corridor toward the Felt Forum, with most of the people going in the opposite direction. They looked like harmless, happy cat fanciers. A few of them carried cats in cages, but under close scrutiny none of the cats were wearing little sweat socks.

Jane Meara was standing by the entrance to the exhibition hall. She looked like a biker gang had just raped her Cabbage Patch doll.

I introduced Jane to Ratso and the three of us made our way into the hall. The whole place had the air of a carnival that couldn't make up its mind whether or not it was leaving town. All around us people were either packing up their cages or preparing their cats for last-minute judging. Every few moments someone would race by with a cat on his upturned palm like an Italian waiter with a rush-order pizza.

Rocky's empty cage had food, water, a litter box, a bed, and lace curtains. If the rents kept going up, I might check in there myself.

Rocky seemed very gone indeed.

A woman came up beside us wringing her hands. 'This is terrible,' she said. 'I'm Marilyn Park, the producer of the show. This is the first time anything like this has happened at one of our shows. I know how you must feel, Jane, dear.'

Jane nodded and let go with a little sob.

'Look, Miss Park – ' I said.

'*Mrs* Park,' said Mrs. Park. 'My husband and I produce the shows together and I told Stanley security here at the Garden should've been tighter.'

'Mrs Park – ' I said.

'Call me Marilyn,' she said. 'And we *will* find the cat. We have people checking right now into all the places a lost little pussycat could go.'

'Marilyn,' I said, 'do you think the cat is loose in the Garden or do you think someone could've *taken* Rocky?'

'All the cats,' she said, 'have identification numbers. They're checked coming in and leaving the exhibition hall.'

'Well,' I said, 'do you think . . .'

I stopped.

Something was winking at me from beneath the lace curtains in the corner of the cage. It was too short to be a Times Square hooker. It was too small even to be a cat. I reached into the cage, put my hand under the curtains, and withdrew a metal object.

It was the key to room 407 of the Roosevelt Hotel.

I turned the key over in my hand. I put my arm around Jane Meara.

'I don't think Rocky's in the Garden,' I said.

The cab ride over to the Roosevelt was a bit strained. Jane appeared to be fighting off a mounting hysteria. Ratso was behaving like a self-appointed member of a lost-cat support group.

'We'll find him, Jane,' he said. 'We'll find him.'

'He's a her,' wailed Jane.

'Don't worry,' said Ratso. 'There ain't a cat alive that the Kinkster can't find . . .'

'That's what I'm worried about!' sobbed Jane. 'Whether she's alive!'

'. . . blindfolded,' continued Ratso, in a stubborn, almost toneless voice.

I was trying not to listen to them. I was trying to think. Why would someone want to steal Jane Meara's cat? I couldn't make head or tail of it.

Marilyn Park had told us that the Roosevelt Hotel was where all the out-of-town cats were staying for the cat show. Almost a thousand of them. One of the few hotels in the city that allowed cats.

As we got out of the cab in front of the Roosevelt, I looked up at the hotel. It looked like a giant gray ship in a children's book, and I imagined hundreds of little cat faces staring

10

down at us from the portholes. I wondered what was waiting for us in room 407.

We crossed the hotel lobby and took the elevator to the fourth floor. Room 407 was down the hall to the left. The hallway was gray, dusty, and smelled like buildings used to smell when you were a child.

I knocked sharply on 407.

Nothing. Not even a meow.

I inserted the key into the lock and opened the door. I hit the lights and we took a look around. The room was not quite empty.

On the bed was a note scrawled on Roosevelt Hotel stationery.

It read: 'What's the matter – cat got your tongue?'

5

We put Jane Meara into a cab. Exposure to a distraught woman was not healthy for Kinky. And my increasing surliness wasn't likely to calm Jane's heart. Somewhere there was a guy who could comfort her. A guy who could take her in his arms and tell her, 'Don't worry, honey, everything's going to be all right.' Unfortunately, the guy probably sang in the Gay Men's Chorus.

Ratso and I crossed Forty-fifth at Madison, took a left, and walked halfway up the block to JR Tobacco, home of the Jamaican 'A' cigar. The Jamaican 'A' has been aged for one full year. The cigar has more breeding than some people I know.

'Scratch one tabby,' said Ratso moments later as the two of us were walking down Fifth Avenue smoking our Jamaican 'A's.' 'Eighty-six one mange-ridden mouser.'

'Not particularly spoken like a cat fancier,' I said.

'I hate the precious, preening, putrid little bastards.'

11

I took a puff on the cigar as we walked along the avenue in the cold. 'They speak very highly of you,' I said.

'I mean it,' said Ratso, poking the air vehemently with his cigar. 'I hate the little bastards.'

'You're not alone,' I said. 'Brahms used to shoot them from his window with a bow and arrow. Napoleon hated cats as well.'

'The French hate everyone.'

'Except Jerry Lewis. Hitler hated cats, too.'

'He wasn't real partial to Jews, either,' said Ratso.

'No,' I said.

We walked along in silence at a fairly brisk pace until we got to Thirty-fifth Street. I pointed to the right in the general vicinity of some old brownstones. 'That's where Nero Wolfe lives,' I said.

Before Ratso could say anything, a dark blur shot through the street directly across our path. A black cat.

Ratso made a hard right up my leg and tried to nest in my vest pocket. I didn't think he was a Nero Wolfe devotee, so I had to assume that he was avoiding the path of the black cat. Couldn't blame him.

We were only a few blocks from the Garden and I felt I would be remiss in my responsibilities as a friend and country-singer-turned-amateur-detective if I didn't go back and look for Rocky one more time. Not that I figured we'd find anything.

I bribed Ratso to come along with me to the Garden. I offered him three cigars and promised I'd buy lunch next time at Big Wong, our favorite Chinese restaurant. It was almost shameful to have to tempt an adult in this way, but as Ratso pointed out, he hardly knew Jane Meara, and his dislike of cats was long-standing and rather intense. It would've been useless to try to reason with him.

In fact, the whole little affair didn't seem to be making a

12

hell of a lot of sense. Somebody, it would appear, was playing a pretty mean prank on Jane Meara. And Jane Meara was the kind of person who didn't have an enemy in the world. Never much liked that kind of person myself. Still, I couldn't imagine hating her. Evidently, someone could and did.

Or maybe it was Rocky they were after. But Rocky, from what I understood, was more of a house pet than a grand champion. Outside of her four little sweat socks, there wasn't much about her that would whip your average cat fancier into a sexual frenzy. Of course, cat fanciers had been known to have rather strange appetites. Stranger even than the menu at Big Wong.

We got to Eighth Avenue and entered through the side doors of the Felt Forum. It was nudging nine o'clock and there was a steady stream of cage-carrying cat fanciers and assorted spectators leaving the Garden area. We had almost gotten to the entrance of the exhibition hall when I noticed a worrisome knot of people gathered in a corner off to the left-hand side of the lobby. At the center of the small crowd stood a big, burly man with a little notebook.

He looked unpleasantly familiar.

A large woman carrying a large cat in a large cage blocked my field of vision for a moment. When she stepped out of the way, I caught a brief but sufficient glimpse of the mal-evolent mug of Detective Sergeant Mort Cooperman from the Sixth Precinct. Sufficient to remind me that Cooperman and I were not exactly chummy. And sufficient to tell me that something was terribly wrong at the cat show.

If they'd found Rocky, somehow I didn't think it was going to be pretty. I was glad Jane Meara wasn't around.

'Ratso,' I said, 'I think we're too late.'

'Too late? What do you mean?'

'I mean I think we've got a dead cat on the line.'

13

When you look for something in life, sometimes you find it. Then you find it wasn't what you were looking for. Then you wonder why the hell you went looking for it in the first place. Just curiosity, you figure. You rack your brains trying to remember what curiosity did to the cat. Did it make him healthy, wealthy, and wise? Did it help him get the worm? Oh, Christ! It killed him!

But by now it's too late. You catch your reflection in a stolen hubcap – you're a cat. The specter of curiosity, which looks like a large, seductive venetian blind, stalks you across miles and miles of bathroom tiles ... across the cold and creaky warehouse floor of your life ... across a candlelit table in a restaurant that closed twelve years ago. Shut down by the city for being too quaint.

I killed what was left of the Jamaican 'A' and Ratso and I walked across the foyer to where the people were standing. We were just in time to hear Marilyn Park say to Sergeant Cooperman, 'Nothing like this has ever happened at one of our shows.'

Ratso nodded solemnly and winked at me. I watched the man standing next to Marilyn Park, a shadowy fellow whom I took to be her husband, Stanley Park. The one who thought the security at the show was adequate. He was introducing a third man to Cooperman.

'Sergeant,' said Stanley Park, 'this gentleman is Hilton Head. He's in charge of all our public relations. The spokesperson for the whole show.'

Head was a nervous, rather effeminate young man who ran a limp hand through limp hair and kept repeating the phrase '... such a pussycat ... such a pussycat ...'

Cooperman glowered at the young man and scribbled a thing or two in his little notebook. You can always tell a cop with a notebook from an angry young novelist with a note-book. Both of them are angry, but the novelist opens his notebook from the side while the cop flips the pages over the top.

Cooperman flipped a page over the top and looked up from his notebook. He was not pleased to see me standing there in the small crowd of cat fanciers.

He tried to pick me up by the scruff of the neck with his left eye.

'Jesus Christ,' he said, 'talk about a bad penny.'

'Did you find the cat?' I asked.

'Did we find the cat?' said Cooperman with a smile. 'Yeah, we found the cat.'

'Where's the cat now?' I asked.

'Where's the cat now? The cat's right back here in this office.' He jerked his thumb toward what looked like a small cloakroom.

Cooperman had a fairly sick smile on his face that I couldn't quite cipher. I wasn't sure I wanted to.

'Wanna take a look?' he asked.

I shrugged and motioned to Ratso and the two of us followed his trucklike body into the small room adjoining the foyer. At first I didn't see anything because a camera flash went off practically right in my eyes. When I could see, I couldn't believe what I was seeing. The room was a beehive of activity. Cops and technicians all over the place. Rocky was nowhere in sight. But something else was.

On the floor in the center of the room was the body of a man. His chest was so red it looked like ET's little heart-light.

There was a blood-encrusted, gaping hole where you kind of expected a mouth to be.

'How do you like that?' said Sergeant Cooperman cheer-fully. 'Looks like the cat's lost his tongue.'

If life is but a dream, death is but a nightmare. That information notwithstanding, I was pleased to find, when I woke up Tuesday morning, that my cat was still in the loft and my tongue was still in my head. All things considered, not a bad way to start the day.

I fed the cat, put the espresso machine into high gear, and lit my first cigar of the morning. I looked out the window at the sun-dappled, grimy warehouses across the street. The billboards were glistening with dew. The rust was shining on all the fire escapes. It was a beautiful morning.

I sat down at the kitchen table for a quiet cup of espresso. If you ignored the constant rumbling of the garbage trucks, everything was fairly peaceful. One of the appealing things about this case, I reflected, was that a dead man with his tongue cut out couldn't give you any lip.

I sipped the espresso from my Imus in the Morning coffee cup. I puffed the cigar and watched a blue wreath drift upward toward the lesbian dance class. Pretty quiet up there just now. Maybe they were getting into their little lesbian leotards. Or out of them. The whole world loves a lesbian, I thought, and nobody knows dick about her. Of course, when you've got 'em thudding on your ceiling all day long, even lesbians can lose a little magic.

If lesbians were a mystery, so was the dead man at the Garden. But I knew a little more about him. Just a little more. His name was Rick 'Slick' Goldberg. He had a cat entered in the cat show. When he hadn't been busy entering cats in cat shows, he'd been a literary agent.

I had not gotten this information from Sergeant Cooperman. When I'd asked him who the dead man was, he'd asked me if I was next of kin. I'd told him I didn't know because I didn't know who the dead man was. He'd told me to wait till tomorrow and ask a newsboy. That was that.

But if you hang around a few crime scenes you usually learn a thing or two, besides not to hang around crime scenes. Once you get behind the police lines into the crime scene search area, it is assumed that you belong there. Like being backstage at a rock concert – once you're actually there, nobody questions your presence. So I'd gotten the information from a uniform who was standing there listening to his hair grow.

I poured myself another cup of espresso and thought it over. Rick 'Slick' Goldberg. Cat fancier. Literary agent. Current occupation: worm bait. Nothing too slick about worm bait – we're all worm bait waiting to happen. It's what you do while you wait that matters.

Unless you wanted to count my laundry, there were only two things that I needed to do at the moment: find out all I could about the tongueless stiff at the Garden, and find out who'd occupied room 407 at the Roosevelt Hotel yesterday. I decided to call the Roosevelt Hotel.

Rick 'Slick' Goldberg would keep.

8

'Good morning,' said the blower on the left, 'Roosevelt Hotel.'

'Can I speak to the cashier, please?' I said.

'One moment, sir.'

'Fine.'

I waited. I puffed patiently on my cigar as I sat at the desk. I was going to get only one take on this and I knew it'd better be a wrap. I didn't think the 'cat got your tongue' note and the stiff *sans* tongue at the Garden were just one of death's little coincidences. It was past time to turn the note over to Cooperman, but I wanted to take one little shot at the situation first. Maybe I'd hit the side of the barn.

'Cashier,' said an irritated, almost petulant voice. It was the voice of a woman you wouldn't care to meet.

'Mornin', ma'am,' I said in a bright voice. 'This is the FTD florist in Fort Worth. Chuck speakin'.' Try to disarm her with a little southern charm. I thought briefly of how John Kennedy had once described Washington, DC: 'Northern charm and southern efficiency.'

'Yes?' she said impatiently.

'We're havin' a little booger of a problem down here, ma'am. I thought like maybe you could help us with it.'

'Yes?' Sounded like she was warming up to me.

'Seems we sent our Silver Anniversary Cup Bouquet – it's been a real popular item for us – we've got a lot of retired folks down here . . .'

'Sir . . .'

'. . . sent it out yesterday mornin' to a Mrs Rose Bush from here in Texas – I think they said she was related to the Vice President – second cousin or somethin' like that . . .'

'Sir! What exactly do you want?'

'Well, now, we sent it to Mrs Bush – to her room there at the Roosevelt Hotel – and somebody signed for it and took it and now I hear from the boss that Mrs Bush never did get it. Boss's madder'n an Indian who's trying to take a peepee and can't find a teepee.'

There was a silence on the line. Finally, the cashier asked in a rather curt voice, 'What room was the – uh – Bush party in, sir?'

'Well now, let's see . . . The Silver Anniversary Cup Bouquet was sent to – hold the weddin', I'll find it – here it is – room 407.'

'Just a moment, sir.' There was a pause while the cashier

checked her ledger. 'There must be a mistake, sir. There's no Bush party registered.'

'Well, I'll be hog-tied and branded.'

'Will that be all, sir?'

'Well, now, you see, if I could get the name of the party that *was* registered in that room – just for our records, you see – I'd be off the hook. As the catfish said to Little Black Sambo.'

There was a deep and somewhat disgusted sigh on the other end of the line. Then a silence. Then an abrupt decision was apparently made. 'The party registered in room 407 was not from Texas,' said the cashier in an almost haughty voice. 'The party was from Connecticut. The party's name was Fred Katz.'

I took a thoughtful puff on my cigar. 'Care to spell that?' I asked.

9

They say that death is just nature's way of telling you to slow down a little bit. Whether or not that is true, it can certainly add a slightly bitter taste to your espresso.

I listened to the lesbian dance class starting up over my head and I listened to some of the darker thoughts dancing around inside my head. Somehow I did not think that Fred Katz was related to Winnie Katz. In fact, I doubted that he was related to anyone. I doubted that he existed.

The name was obviously a rather humorous alias. Or at least it might've been if Rocky hadn't been missing. And if they hadn't found a stiff in the Garden with his clapper torn out. Little things like that can kill a laugh pretty quickly.

I thought over the whole situation. Somebody's cat was missing and somebody's literary agent had gone to Jesus. Which was more important depended on how you looked at the world. In the case at hand, however, the cat and the agent were closely interrelated. Whoever'd heisted the cat had written the note, and whoever'd written the note had iced the agent. He'd probably done a few other things, too. Could've picked up sticks. Buckled his shoe. Well, whatever he'd done and whoever he was, he had to be declawed and neutered fairly rapidly or things could get ugly.

The first step, I decided, was to drop by the Sixth Precinct and lay the 'cat got your tongue' note on Sergeant Cooperman. It promised to be an extremely tedious little visit, but if I didn't go soon, I might be obstructing a lot more than my own slim likelihood of having a nice day.

I had not forgotten about Marilyn Park, Stanley Park, Hilton Head, and the hundreds of other cat fanciers down at the Garden. They'd be there all week. I hadn't forgotten that an agent like Rick 'Slick' Goldberg had probably made a lot of enemies over the years. If he was like most agents I knew, half his clients would've like to have croaked him.

I remembered a little story my pal John Mankiewicz had told me about a writer in LA who came home to find his house burned to the ground. A neighbor came over and said, 'Your agent came by. He raped your wife and daughter, killed your dog, and torched the whole house.' The writer was stunned. He stumbled through the ashes of his home and all he could say was 'My agent came by?'

I'd put on my hat, coat, and hunting vest, stuffed the note in the vest pocket, left the cat in charge, and was almost out the door when the phones rang. This was good for two reasons: one, I'd forgotten my cigars; and two, it was one of those calls that can change your life. I went back to the desk, picked up a few cigars, and collared the blower on the left.

'Start talkin',' I said.

'Kinky!'

'Yeah.'

'This is Eugene at Jane Meara's office. I'm her assistant.'
Jane, I knew, was an editor now for a large publishing
house.

'Yeah?'

'Jane would like you to come over here right away if you
can.'

The cat had jumped up on the desk, and as I stroked her,
a little shiver went jogging down my spine. 'What seems to
be the problem, Eugene?'

'Well, this may sound crazy – like something out of
Agatha Christie – but Jane just got back from lunch and
there's – '

'Get to the meat of it,' I said irritably.

'There's a butcher knife on her desk. It's covered with
blood.'

I stroked the cat one more time and tried to collect my
thoughts. I fitted the last cigar into the little stitched pocket
of the hunting vest.

'Sharp move,' I said.

10

I took the Otis box to the seventeenth floor of Jane's
building, bootlegging a lit cigar the whole way. Things
didn't get ugly till fourteen, when a woman with a hyper-
sensitive beezer got on and sniffed me out. Nothing last
forever.

I escaped into a small lobby and practically ran into the
back of a tall, snakelike figure who'd been doing a fair
impersonation of a man studying gourmet cookbooks in a
glass showcase. The figure uncoiled and sprang toward me
just as the elevator doors closed.

'What took you so long, Tex?' it hissed. It was Detective Sergeant Buddy Fox, Sixth Precinct.

'Waitin' for my nails to dry,' I said. Fox was probably my second favorite American. My first was everybody else.

'I understand,' said Fox, 'you been squirrelin' some evidence in a homicide. Maybe you oughta fork over this purloined letter we been hearin' so much about. Or would you like to hang on to it till Valentine's Day?' There was a smile on Fox's face but it seemed to lack a certain warmth.

I reached into my vest pocket and handed him the note that Ratso, Jane, and I had found in room 407 of the Roosevelt Hotel.

Dear Jane, I thought. Dear, sweet, innocent, little cat-loving Jane. Right then I could've killed Jane Meara with a pair of numb-nuts, or whatever they're called. Any exotic North Korean martial-arts device would probably do. She'd gotten me into this mess by appealing to a sense of compassion I didn't even know I had. Now, albeit unwittingly, she'd thrown me to the dogs, pigs, jackals, lions, wolves – whatever animal you'd choose if you could be any animal you wanted to be. As for myself, I felt like a swallow that had gone down the wrong way and stopped at a service station for directions to Capistrano. I needed either a road map or a Heimlich maneuver and I wasn't sure which.

Fox escorted me down a maze of hallways to a small office. He motioned for me to go in, stuck his head in the doorway after me, winked, and said, 'Wait here, Tex.'

I looked around the room. There was a sofa and a cluttered desk. On the wall were various book jackets. There was a little bulletin board with pictures of Jane Meara at a baseball game and several shots of a cat. I noticed rather grimly that the cat was wearing four little sweat socks. Rocky. I took down one of the snapshots of Rocky and slipped it into my pocket.

I didn't need Frank and Joe Hardy to tell me I was in Jane Meara's office. I looked carefully at the desk. I did not see a bloody butcher's knife. Of course, it's a little hard to see one if it's sticking in your back.

Actually, I thought, it was nobody's fault. Self-pity could be an important trait in a country singer, but in a detective, it was about as attractive as a busted valise. Maybe the whole, rather tedious situation was just one of the little tricks God plays on us from time to time. Like being born with freckles or coming back from Vietnam on a skateboard.

I was pondering this when a large, vaguely evil form darkened the doorway behind me. Without acknowledging my presence, Cooperman walked around the desk and sat in the chair. Fox slithered across the threshold and motioned me seductively toward the sofa. I walked over and sat down. Still not looking at me, Cooperman took a pack of Gauloises from his pocket, shook one out, and lit it with his Zippo lighter. I took out a cigar and lit it with a Bic. Nobody said anything. If silence was golden, we were closing in on the Klondike.

11

An hour and a half later I was ready to bring my brain over to the French cleaner's and tell the head frog I wanted light starch. I'd given Cooperman everything I had on room 407 at the Roosevelt Hotel, which was not a hell of a lot. He'd wanted the key to the room and to know precisely how I'd wheedled the name Fred Katz from the desk at the Roosevelt Hotel. 'I have my methods,' I'd said. He was not pleased.

Things went downhill from there.

Cooperman warned me off the case. He told me I could go and look for all the stray pussy I wanted but this was a homicide. Not a missing cat. Once I left this office, he said,

23

he did not wish to see me for at least a couple of years. Maybe three or four.

I got up to go and he said, 'We're not through with you yet.' I sat back down on the sofa and puffed on my second cigar. The cigar was well past the midway point already. I didn't like to smoke a cigar too far past the midway point, but then I didn't like a lot of things. Cooperman, for instance.

I asked Cooperman about the knife and he told me it was already at the lab. Knowing what he did *now*, he said pointedly, he had little doubt that it was the murder weapon.

It was at about this time that Cooperman had Jane Meara brought in, sat her down next to me on the sofa, and told her in very graphic terms for the first time exactly how the charming implement had been employed prior to its arrival upon her desk. She hadn't even known about the stiff, much less the tongue, and she turned white as a Klansman on the Fourth of July.

Cooperman asked her another question but he got no answer. When you pay your nickel you're supposed to get a nickel ride. All Cooperman got was an autistic stare.

Cooperman killed his fifth Gauloise in the ashtray. I began the pre-ignition procedures on my third cigar. It wasn't really a contest, of course, but I liked to keep up my end of things. The conversation had begun to lag a bit.

At a signal from Cooperman, Fox went out into the hallway and brought in Jim Landis, the publisher Jane worked for, and Eugene, her assistant editor. Cooperman asked Landis where he'd been for the past few hours. Landis said he'd been at a nearby restaurant. Fox took the name of the place and said he'd check it out.

Eugene said he'd been at his desk all through the lunch hour and several authors and would-be authors had stopped by Jane's office while she was out. He had their names on memo slips at his desk.

'Would you be so kind as to bring them to us now?' Cooperman asked in a sweet, sarcastic voice. Eugene went out with Fox. I smoked my cigar. Jane sniffed quietly next to me. Landis fidgeted. Cooperman glared at the empty doorway.

Eugene came back and handed the memos to Cooperman. Cooperman handed them to Fox. 'That's it?' he asked.

Eugene nodded. Then he seemed to remember something. 'Oh, wait,' he said, 'there were some people here right after you left, Jane. They said they were from the cat show and they wanted – '

'Cat show?' said Cooperman.

'Cat show,' said Eugene.

'Names?' asked Cooperman.

'I – I didn't get their names,' said Eugene. He was starting to wither visibly.

'You didn't get their names!' shouted Cooperman.

'Well – they said they'd be back to see Jane. I didn't think – is it important?'

'No,' said Cooperman, 'it's not important. We're just here having a little fun at the office today. We're playing visitor trivia.'

With a snarl, Cooperman gestured viciously toward Eugene and shouted, 'Fox! Take this guy outa my sight and get descriptions.'

Cooperman picked up his cigarettes, waved Landis out with his hand, and told Jane Meara she could have her office back. Jane shuddered. Cooperman stood up. I stood up. Cooperman looked at me. His eyes were a curious admixture of pity, malice, and maybe something just a little more unsavory.

'Penny for your thoughts,' I said.

25

Cooperman gave out a dry, gritty chuckle. Sounded like a guy trying to start his lawn mower in 1957.

'I'll be seeing you around, Tex,' he said.

12

Tuesday night. Ten o'clock. Ratso and I walked into the Carnegie Delicatessen, our home away from home away from home. It smelled great – like pastrami and perfume, salami and cigars. The Carnegie warmed your heart like a matzo ball in January and that, in fact, was what I had my dial set on when we walked into the place. Matzo ball soup with a matzo ball about the size of McGovern's head. McGovern was my friend who wrote for the *Daily News* and sometimes, rather grudgingly, helped me gather crucial data on various and nefarious individuals. McGovern had the largest head in North America.

Leo met Ratso and me at the door like a white Joe Louis. He owned the Carnegie, but his greetings were so effusive he could've fooled you. He was equally enthusiastic even if you'd just been in the place that same afternoon. Of course, I hadn't been in Leo's place. I'd been in Sergeant Cooperman's face.

'Kinky! Kinky!' said Leo, as he rushed over and took my hand warmly in both of his own. Shucking all modesty, I had to admit that very few patrons were greeted in this warm a fashion. Several customers looked up from their blintzes.

'When you playin' at the Lone Star again, Kinky?' Leo asked.

'Well, not for a while Leo, if I can help it,' I said to the back of Leo's head. He'd turned away from me to greet Ratso. Probably asking him how the magazine was going. Maybe admiring his wardrobe. I passed the awkward

26

moment admiring the salamis in the window and presently Leo's attention turned back to me. Patience is always rewarded.

'So Kinky,' said Leo, 'so how's the Broadway musical coming along?' I had written the score for a Broadway musical comedy but my collaborator, Don Imus, had been dragging his feet on the book for about four years. Lately, Imus had been showing a little bit of progress.

'Yeah . . . well,' I said unenthusiastically, 'we hope to have a few homosexuals tapdancing by late summer.'

'Great, Kinky!' said Leo. 'Great.'

Leo called a waiter over and got us a table. As Ratso and I sat down we heard Leo, in the best tradition of the stage whisper, shout to the waiter, 'Give 'em linen!'

Ratso and I were seated across from each other in the middle of a long table, with people on both sides of us. The guy on my immediate right was so close that when he ate his smoked fish I could spit out the bones. Everybody at the table had paper napkins with the Carnegie logo: a picture of Leo holding a tray and saying, 'I make a goooood sandwich.' I ordered seltzer and coffee and began looking over the miles of menu. Ratso began working on the bucket of pickles that was always on the table. Then the waiter brought our linen.

It created a mild ripple effect. A bit of whispering. A nervous chuckle here and there. A little resentment. A look of wonder on one lady's face before she went back to her chopped liver. I put my linen napkin on my lap but Ratso, in an embarrassingly ostentatious gesture, tucked his into the neck of his shirt like a lobster bib. Each to his own, I thought.

But mainly, it felt good. In fact, it felt goooood.

Possibly very few people attach as much importance as I do to being given a linen napkin at the Carnegie Delicatessen. Most people, of course, spend their lives caring about the wrong things. They worry about South Africa or Nicaragua. They spend so much time finding themselves that they lose their taxicabs. They don't see that what kind of napkin you get at a delicatessen is a matter of much significance in the world today.

That's why they don't get linen.

I'd knocked off a bowl of matzo ball soup and Ratso had eaten an obscenely large piece of gefilte fish and a pope's nose, which isn't obscene but should be because it's a turkey's ass. We were both still hungry. Ratso studied his menu like a handicapper looking at a racing form.

'A little more interesting crowd's starting to drift in here now,' I said. 'They look like either theatrical types or hookers.'

'Or Puerto Ricans from the United Nations,' Ratso said, looking up from his menu. 'So tell me about the investigation.'

I told Ratso about Fred Katz. I told Ratso about the bloody butcher knife. I told Ratso about the cat show people who had come by Jane Meara's office while she was out. I told Ratso I couldn't make up my mind what else to order.

'So what're you going to do?' Ratso asked.

'I don't know,' I said. 'I'm caught between corned beef and pastrami.' I looked at the menu.

'I'm talkin' about the case,' said Ratso. 'What're you going to do about the case?'

'Nothing,' I said. 'Sergeant Cooperman warned me off.'

'Ah, c'mon,' said Ratso, dismissing the issue with a wave of a pickle. 'You're not gonna let a little thing like that stop you, are you? This is America. This is 1988.' He took another bite of the pickle and thought about it for a moment. 'This is the Carnegie Deli,' he said.

'I know all that,' I said. 'I just don't want to think about it right now. All I want to think about is what I want to order.' I looked down at the menu again.

Leo hovered in from the left like a Huey chopper, with his rotors rotating. 'Kinky! How ya doin', Kinky? What can I get you?'

'I don't know, Leo,' I said. 'I'm somewhat confused as to what to order.'

'I know the perfect thing,' said Leo. 'I'll be right back. Just a moment.'

He veered off in the general direction of the kitchen. When Leo came back he was holding a large, rather unpleasant-looking, purplish object.

'Here,' he said. 'How about I cut you a nice tongue?'

13

That night, back at 199B Vandam, I had a heart-to-heart talk with my cat. I was sitting at the desk. The cat was sitting on the desk. So was a bottle of Jameson Irish whiskey and the old bull's horn.

I'd had a few shots. The cat hadn't touched the stuff. Probably pacing herself.

'Have you ever wondered,' I said, 'why Negro undertakers always drive white hearses and white undertakers always drive black hearses?'

The cat looked at me and blinked her eyes.

'I know it's a tough question,' I said. While the cat thought about it I poured another generous slug into the bull's horn. Then I poured the bull's horn into my mouth.

'I'm not afraid to die,' I said. 'I'm not afraid to live. I'm not afraid to fail. I'm not afraid to succeed. I'm not afraid to fall in love. I'm not afraid to be alone. I'm just afraid I might have to stop talking about myself for five minutes.'

The cat yawned.

'It's not easy being who I am,' I said. 'Sometimes I think of myself as a country singer. Sometimes as a Broadway composer . . .'

The cat shook her right front paw in an unmistakable gesture of irritability.

'. . . sometimes as a private dick,' I said.

The cat stood up on the desk and stretched. Starting to get restless. I pretended I didn't notice.

'I'll tell you,' I said, 'it's lonely in the middle.'

On an impulse I picked up the cat and held her close to me. Cats, like everybody else, are a fairly perverse lot. They wish to be held only by those who don't wish to hold them. By the time I remembered this it was too late.

The cat scratched me severely on my right wrist. Then she jumped down and bounded away. I chased her, cornered her, and hit her with my open hand on top of her head. She screamed and ran under the couch. I glanced down at my arm. Looked like a nearly successful adolescent suicide attempt.

'You asshole!' I shouted. The cat had come a little way out from behind the couch so she could enjoy watching me. Technically, I thought, the cat was not an asshole. As my friend Bianca is fond of saying, 'Assholes are people [or cats] who don't know that they're assholes.' By this standard, the cat was not an asshole.

Neither was I.

I went back to the desk and poured another jolt into the bull's horn. There are those who would say, I thought bitterly, that it is not right for a 170–pound man to hit an 8–pound cat. Even with an open hand. It's not fair, they'd say. Hardly the appropriate response to the situation, they'd snivel.

Well, it didn't make me especially proud to be an

American, but you couldn't always turn the other cheek. Life is a game of give and take. Dog eat dog. Cat scratch man. Man hit cat.

Hell, it'd be all right. Couple of days, everything'd be back to merely strange. Anyway, it was none of their goddamn business. It was an act of passion.

I looked down at my wrist. I glared across the room at the cat. It didn't bring me a hell of a lot of satisfaction, though, because the cat had closed her eyes and was curled up asleep in the rocking chair.

I sighed, picked up the bull's horn, killed the shot, and lit a cigar. I watched the smoke drift away and disappear like the dreams of a child who always wanted to be a fireman.

14

Wednesday morning I was doing a pretty good impersonation of a busy little New Yorker. I had the espresso machine, a cigar, and the blower on the left all going simultaneously. Somewhere out there was a lost cat. Somewhere out there was a killer. My plan, with or without the help of the police, was to find them both. If you had to have an impossible dream, you might as well make it a good one.

On the other end of the line, Jane Meara was telling me how sorry she was to have landed me in hot water with the police.

'They told me to tell them *everything*,' she said.

'Forget it,' I said. 'I'm still on the case, in spite of Cooperman's warning.'

'Kinky,' she said falteringly, 'I don't think–'

'This is America,' I said. 'This is 1988.'

'This dangerous.'

31

'I like danger. It gives me a buzz. It's supposed to be good aerobically.' I puffed a few times on the cigar.

'It was horrible about Slick,' she said. 'You know, I had lunch with him that same afternoon.'

'Didn't know that. What'd you talk about?'

'Oh, just the usual. The big deals he was working on. Who he was touting this week.'

'Who was he touting this week?'

'Oh, some guy who'd written a book about how there's an inordinate number of mass murderers who have the middle name Wayne. The author feels that their fathers overidentified with John Wayne, named their sons accordingly, and thus passed along a sort of festering internalized violence as well.'

'Coffee table job?'

'No. It's a long-winded psychological tome. I passed.'

'So did Slick,' I said. I paused to glance over at the espresso machine. It looked and sounded like it was preparing to fly to Jupiter. 'What kind of guy was Slick?' I asked.

'Well,' said Jane, 'he wasn't particularly well loved.'

'Apparently not,' I said.

Jane put in a fast plug for finding Rocky, said she had to run, and then we ciao-ed off. I beat a path to the espresso machine, poured a cup, went back to my desk, sat down, and took a sip. It was a lot of work for that hour of the morning.

I leaned back in the chair and thought about agents. Agents were people, too. Just like cats. Maybe not quite as thoughtful or sensitive sometimes. But who was?

Pieces were beginning to fall together. For one thing, the person who called himself Fred Katz had quite conceivably never occupied room 407 at the Roosevelt. He'd just left the 'cat got your tongue' note there and headed for the Garden to take Rocky, leave the room key in the cage, and dispense with Slick Goldberg. That would make for a busy afternoon and it didn't leave a lot of time to decide what to do with Rocky before inking Slick's final deal. Of course he could've taken Rocky back to the hotel, but how would he get into the room without a key? And obtaining two keys, under the circumstances, would've risked arousing the desk clerk's suspicion. So Rocky must've been set loose on the street or dispatched to kitty heaven in a rather rapid fashion. It'd be too big an order to kill the agent without letting the cat out of the bag, so to speak.

I took a deep breath and called McGovern at the *Daily News.*

'National Desk,' said a familiar voice.

'Yeah, National Desk,' I said, 'I'd like to report a runaway garden slug out here in Westchester.'

'Is it an exclusive?' McGovern asked.

'McGovern,' I said, 'this is Kinky. I need a favor.'

'No shit,' he said. I took a patient puff on my cigar. It was important that McGovern not go into a snit. If he did, it could be unpleasant.

'It's really a small thing,' I said, 'but you could get it done a lot faster than I could. You've got the connections. Besides, I'm working on a case and I've got to be somewhere soon.'

'Where do you have to be?'

'The cat show at Madison Square Garden.'

There was no response.

'All I want is for you to place an ad in the *Daily News* for a lost cat.'

There was a stunned silence on the line. It was followed by hearty, incredulous Irish laughter. McGovern was one of the few people in the world who, even when being incredulous, could be hearty. He was always Irish.

I figured I'd rush him with the ad copy while he was still laughing. 'Okay,' I said, 'it runs like this: "Fred Katz – all is forgiven. Return Rocky and no questions will be asked. Call Kinky – 555–3717." '

'You know,' said McGovern, 'I'm a little disappointed in you. Just a *little* disappointed.' He laughed again.

'What's the big deal?' I asked. 'I'm busy this morning and I thought – '

'I've covered every beat there is,' said McGovern with some intensity. 'I got the exclusive on the Richard Speck murders in Chicago. I spent six weeks covering Charles Manson. I got the most in-depth story ever on Lieutenant Calley. . . .'

'Rusty?'

'Yeah,' said McGovern, 'good ol' Rusty. I've spent over two decades covering major news stories. My whole career – my whole life – has been building, building up to this moment, when a country singer I know calls me to place a want ad for a lost cat. Kind of makes it all worthwhile.'

Dealing with McGovern had turned out to be at least as tedious as calling *Daily News* advertising and placing the ad myself, which I should have done in the first place. But you dance with who brung you.

'So you'll do it,' I said. I waited.

'Sure, ol' pal,' said McGovern a bit wistfully.

'Thanks, pal,' I said. 'You're a great American.'

'You could do me a little favor, too,' said McGovern.

'Sure,' I said, 'what is it?'

'You can tell the Pulitzer committee they can go back to bed now,' he said.

That afternoon Ratso and I went to the Garden to weed out a killer. Ratso had taken a renewed interest, indeed a fascination, in the case from the moment he'd seen the stiff. Death is a hot ticket. For rubberneckers on an expressway viewing a tragic accident or for would-be Watsons, the specter of death is compelling. It requires the subtlety of a more Sherlockian mind to appreciate the finding of a lost cat.

That morning, before I'd left the loft, I'd spoken to Eugene in Jane Meara's office, described the people I planned to interview at the Garden, and discovered, not to my total wonderment, that the cat show visitors to Jane's office bore a strong similarity to Marilyn and Stanley Park and their spokesperson, Hilton Head. Of course, they could've been Marilyn and Stanley Park and Hilton Head impersonators, but somehow I rather doubted it.

I assigned Ratso to plague the three of them with his presence. I told him to insinuate himself into their lives and find out all there was to know. For myself, I had other ideas.

I figured I would start in the area of Rocky's disappearance, talk to people and cats, absorb the ambience of the place. Where was Rocky? What made the Cheshire Cat smile? What made some people kill? I wanted to know more about cats in general. More about God and man. Less about William Buckley.

The Garden looked spectral as Ratso and I got out of the cab, almost evil. The afternoon was cold as blue eyes that didn't love you anymore. It was starting to rain.

I grudgingly paid the driver, who was allergic to cigar smoke and probably a number of other things. Pretty smart to get a job driving a hack in New York City if you're allergic to cigar smoke. Of course, as a child, the driver probably hadn't wanted to be an allergy-prone cab driver. No child wants to be that. Just as no child wants to grow up to be a critic for *The New York Times*. Children want to be something good and meaningful in life. Like the fire chief of Spokane.

I lit a cigar and Ratso and I walked silently through the gray day like two mothmen drawn to the bright flames of death.

I walked around in the Garden for a while, focusing on the vague area where Rocky'd disappeared two days earlier. I combed the area thoroughly and didn't come up with as much as an ear mite. Every time I saw a receptive face I'd take out the snapshot I'd liberated from Jane Meara's office and ask the person. 'Ever seen this cat?'

None of them recognized Rocky. However, once I identified the cat as Rocky, many of them commented on her abduction. No one seemed to think the cat could have wandered off. No one had seen anyone strange hanging around.

Of course, the cat owners themselves were such a strange-looking lot it would've been hard to notice anyone who had looked strange.

I was about ready to call in the dogs as it were, piss on the fire, and go find Ratso, when I saw her.

She was wearing a David Copperfield cap and between her hands she was stretching what appeared to be a large white rat. Beneath the cap her face looked beautiful and vaguely ethnic in a childlike, poignant, American kind of way, like a parade in New York for a country that, for all practical purposes, no longer existed.

She looked half of something pretty weird and I just hoped it wasn't Turkish. Their only major export was knives that went around corners.

36

'Sexy weather we're havin',' I said. I'd gotten that one from a male cab driver one rainy evening at the Vancouver Airport.

'What do you want?' she asked.

'Well, I don't want what's between your hands,' I said.

She smiled a mischievous smile and turned a beautiful, cold shoulder to me. She carried the large white rat over to a table and placed him on it. Like a confused Pied Piper, I followed the rat.

I stopped a little distance away and looked at the two of them. The rat still looked like a rat, but the broad looked like a killer. What the hell, I thought, I was looking for a killer.

We carried on a rather strained cocktail conversation without the cocktails and I learned a number of things. Her name was Leila. She was half Palestinian. She was a judge at the cat show. She had not been holding a large white rat. She'd been holding a purebred hairless Sphynx. She'd heard of Rocky's disappearance and she'd read about the murder in the newspaper, but she could offer no new information about either. The last thing I learned was that she did not wish to join me for a drink.

I caught up with Ratso right in front of a veterinarian giving a slide show on diarrhea. Ratso was having a rather animated discussion with Hilton Head. I walked up just in time to hear Head say, 'I hope you're satisfied!' and to see him prance away.

'There goes a very unhappy young man,' I said.

'Yes,' said Ratso, 'and he's gonna miss the rest of the slide show.'

'So are we,' I said.

I would like to be able to say that I felt a slight prickling effect on the back of my neck as Ratso and I started to leave the Garden. It would've been nice if I'd noticed the hairs on the backs of my hands standing up like little Sandinista soldiers. Unfortunately, all I noticed was that I'd spent several hours asking people about some cat many of them had never heard of and daydreaming about a sensitive relationship with a Palestinian harem girl. I didn't know if I'd be seeing Leila again or under what circumstances that event was to occur. I only knew that if I succeeded in tearing away the veil from her heart, the two of us might have a decent chance of erasing six thousand years of bad karma.

'Well, what'd you get, Rats?' I asked as we walked down the hallway from the Felt Forum to the Garden proper.

'Hilton Head is a born-again Christian.'

'Mildly unpleasant.'

'Yeah, and it's kind of funny, too.'

'Why is that?'

"Cause he doesn't look like a born-again Christian.'

I stopped briefly to light a cigar. 'What about Marilyn Park?' I asked.

'She's a vegetarian.'

'Good detective work,' I said as I blew on the end of the cigar. 'Were you able to learn what her favorite color is?'

'No,' said Ratso, 'but I did find out something rather strange about Stanley Park. His wife and Head say that the three of them went by Jane Meara's office yesterday.'

'So?'

'Park says it's the first he's heard of it. Claims he was here supervising the judging all afternoon.'

'Interesting discrepancy.'

'Yeah,' said Ratso. 'So who was the third man? Maybe our old friend Fred Katz?' The only times I'd ever seen Ratso that animated were when somebody else was paying for his lunch.

'Well, you might have something there,' I said. 'Or . . .'

'Or—what?'

'Or . . . nothing.'

'Terrific, Sherlock. I've just discovered what could be a vital clue. What've you turned up?'

We walked out the front doors of the Garden and down the walkway toward Seventh Avenue. I thought about it for a moment. Then I told Ratso about Leila.

'I don't see how your wanting to jump the bones of a female camel jockey is relevant to the case,' he said.

I shrugged. 'She and I could be the last hope for peace in the Middle East,' I said. Ratso was not impressed and responded with a fairly ethnic hand gesture.

We were nearing the end of the walkway when a figure stepped out from behind a portico. It was wearing a garish mask not dissimilar to the ones worn in the Broadway show *Cats*. There was something rather frightening in its manner – like catching a Jekyll entering the on-ramp to Mr Hyde. There was also something rather frightening in its right hand.

It was a gun and it was pointed at my heart.

16

Everybody dies an early death sooner or later. I'd always hoped mine could've been a little later. Dying's not what it's cracked up to be. But in all fairness, very few things are. Body surfing, for one.

The figure adjusted the mask and I adjusted to the notion that I might've gotten linen for the last time. The Jamaican cigar I was holding like a lifeline in my right hand might be the last Jamaican cigar I'd ever smoke. I'd probably never go to Jamaica now. I'd probably never even go to Big Wong.

Funny the things you think about when your life hangs like a stray gray thread on Ratso's Hadassah Thrift Shop coat. Maybe it continues to cling there and you continue to live. Or maybe some well-meaning, neurotic broad puts down her plastic cup of white wine at a SoHo gallery opening and says, 'Just a minute, Ratso, honey, you've got a thread hanging on your coat.' She picks off the thread and you die. The landlord finds a new tenant and raised the rent. The cat goes to the city pound. The girl in the peach-colored dress calls, hears your voice still on the machine, leaves a message, and wonders why you never got back to her. Serves her right for waiting so damn long to call.

Answering machines tend to take on a life of their own. I remember the time the pope called Mother Teresa and told her she was needed in Los Angeles. Mother Teresa thought it was an unusual assignment, but the pope told her there were many poor people in the *barrios* there who needed her help. So, about three months later, the pope called Mother Teresa in LA. She wasn't home but he got her answering machine. The message said, 'Hi. This is Terri. I'm away from the phone right now . . .'

It's amazing how much time you have when you're out of time. Strangled images struggled through Kentucky Fried synapses under my cowboy hat. What used to be. What might have been. A dark and beautiful girl in a little blue car – the prettiest girl in the world with a flower in her hair . . .

And there was Leila. Brown eyes sharing sweet and sour secrets of Semitism. Fragile Arabian ankles I would never be familiar with. I hated to pass the Middle East peace baton back to the Henry Kissingers of the world. Let them try to sleep counting tiny little Cambodians. Soon I would probably be a tiny little Cambodian, too. Any moment now. . . . Leila again . . . Brown eyes . . . as my friend Chinga Chavin says . . . that look like handcuffs . . . And the espresso machine I leave to Ratso . . .

Suddenly the cat behind the mask gave forth with a sharp, chilling sound – half feline, half fiendish – somewhere between a cynical, human meow and the noise a cat would make if it could laugh.

Then it pulled the trigger.

17

When I came to there were two green garden snakes coming out of my stomach and three Ratsos sitting by my bedside. All of them looked hungry. The three Ratsos were eating bagels, and whatever the green garden snakes were eating I didn't want to know, so I went back to sleep.

When I woke up the second time, there was only one Ratso and he was eating a large slice of pizza from John's of Bleecker Street, the best in New York. Ratso ate like a starving boar-hog but he had taste.

'Where are the other two Ratsos?' I asked, I didn't know if it was night or day, but it was beginning to dawn on me that I was in a hospital. Hell would have to wait.

'The other two Ratsos?' he said uncertainly. 'Maybe they're out playing with the other two Kinkys.'

I thought about it for a moment. My mind was clearing a little more slowly than my vision. It took a while to think about the other two Kinkys and the other two Ratsos. 'Maybe they're working on a case,' I said.

'Could be,' said Ratso, nodding his head. 'What kind of case do you think they're working on?'

'Maybe they're finding the little missing children on the milk cartons,' I said.

'Maybe,' said Ratso. I could tell he was worried, because he'd stopped eating his pizza. 'Look, Kinkster,' he said, 'you just rest here a minute. I'm going to go find the doctor.'

Ratso walked out into the hall and I looked around the

41

room. Everything came back to me like a buzzard on the highway. Obviously I'd been shot. Obviously I wasn't dead. Obviously I was in a hospital room. Obviously my friends hadn't sent a hell of a lot of flowers.

The tendrils of my brain were becoming a little less fuzzy and they were damn close to grasping onto something important. I tried to think again and this time I connected. Whoever'd shot me must've know I was at the Garden and must've known what I was looking for. That brought it down to a very small group of people. The Parks. Hilton Head. Leila?

I credited myself with enough native sensitivity to rule out the people I'd shown the Rocky pictures to. I'd seen nothing in their eyes beyond the pale of innocence, sympathy, admiration, boredom – each a normal cat fancier, if such an animal existed. I'd learned to beware of 'normal' and 'harmless' types. It was the 'normal' and 'harmless' types that usually did you in. And the women.

My spirits sagged a bit as I enlarged the field of suspects to practically everybody I'd shown the photograph to and his kid sister. And God knew what Ratso had stirred up interviewing the Parks and Head. It was hopeless. For all I knew the veterinarian could've shot me for walking out of his slide show on diarrhea. Men have been shot for less.

I shook my head, cleared a couple of cobwebs, and my spirits lifted again. There had been something familiar about the figure behind the cat mask. I wasn't sure exactly what it was. I wasn't even certain whether it'd been a man or a woman. But whoever it was, I was very conscious of one thing. It had seemed to know me. That narrowed the field.

I was trying to remember what it was that had been familiar when the doctor came into the room briskly with Ratso tailing after him like a large jet stream. The doctor looked like Robert Young on a bad day. He adjusted a few knobs on something that looked like a sound system, put a stethoscope to what I'm pleased to call my heart, fondled one of the garden snakes, and smiled.

'You had a close call,' he said. 'A very close call. I'm going to keep you here for a few more days.'

'Well,' I said, 'at least we'll find out if my Blue Cross has wheels on it.'

Robert Young laughed the same friendly, hollow laugh that he always used to tag the Sanka commercials with. The nervous window-washer who works on the ninety-seventh floor has just switched to Sanka. Robert Young asks how he's feeling now. He says, 'Great, now that I've switched to Sanka.' Robert Young laughs, ha-ha-ha. You didn't exactly trust that laugh, but it was comforting.

'You know,' he said, coming nicely off the laugh, 'you've been unconscious for over twelve hours.' Of course I hadn't known it. I would've had to be the Three Faces of Kinky to have known it.

'Yeah,' said Ratso, 'you were almost the Rip Van fucking Winkle of the Village.'

I looked at Robert Young. 'Did you get the bullet out?' I asked.

Robert Young looked at me. Then he gave forth with another friendly, indulgent little chuckle. 'There was no bullet,' he said. 'You were shot with a tranquilizer dart.'

'A tranquilizer dart?' I couldn't believe it.

'A tranquilizer dart,' said Robert Young. 'The kind they use on the big cats.'

18

I spent Friday afternoon in a hospital bed dreaming of cigars. But I took a little time out to empathize with a dead literary agent whom nobody had liked and to overidentify with a lost cat whom one person loved.

But then, I was more sensitive than most Americans. In fact, most Americans were more sensitive than most Americans.

I'd had a phone hooked up in the room and I'd been working it like a hyperactive croupier most of the morning. I like telephones. On some occasions, I love telephones. They sometimes make it possible to travel across the darkness in the distance of a dream. I like cats better than agents but I wanted to be fairly scientific about the thing, so I'd begun my calls in alphabetical order; that is, I made the calls pertaining to the dead agent prior to those pertaining to the lost cat. An organized mind solves an organized crime.

I called Esther 'Lobster' Newberg, an agent I knew, and learned the worst. *Everybody* had hated Rick 'Slick' Goldberg. Lobster didn't wish to speak ill of the dead, and she didn't wish to speak ill of other agents (many disgruntled writers would consider this to be the same thing), but even she had not much liked Rick 'Slick' Goldberg. If I could've paged his mother at the Shalom Retirement Village, *she* probably wouldn't've liked Rick 'Slick' Goldberg. Well, it was a murder case, not a popularity contest.

I made another call or two and then called my friend Ted Mann in Hollywood, the glitzy graveyard of all talent. Things were going so poorly, Ted said, that he'd had to hire a non-Jewish agent.

He'd never heard of Rick "Slick' Goldberg, so we talked cats coast-to-coast for a while. Ted said he'd once had a cat named Puss-Puss who'd lived to be twenty-five years old. Outlived most of his friends, he said. When I hung up, it was not without a certain pride. It wasn't the kind of thing you'd really want to crow about, but I *had* outlived Puss-Puss. Of course, a few more tranquilizer-dart incidents like the day before and I might not beat out Puss-Puss by too much.

I was at St Vincent's Hospital, I discovered. According to Robert Young, the contents of the tranquilizer dart had been sent to the lab for analysis. He was eagerly awaiting the results. I told him I was, too. Everybody needs to look forward to something.

Earlier in the afternoon, I'd sent Ratso over to 199B Vandam to get some cigars and fresh clothes, feed the cat, tell her I'd be home soon, and check the messages on the answering machine. It didn't seem like that difficult an assignment, but he still wasn't back. Maybe he'd passed a garage sale on the way.

While I waited for Ratso, I took stock of things. There was only so much you could do from a telephone in a hospital bed. I needed to get out of there before I began relating to Robert Young as a father figure.

But the very fact that I was in a hospital bed and the sequence of events that had put me there were matters of significance in themselves. It all meant that I was getting pretty damn close to whoever it was I was looking for. It also meant that this dart-shooting devil was looking for me. And I had the unpleasant feeling that the hand that had fired the dart had already taken a life, nipped a cat, and severed a tongue.

19

In winter, men's thoughts turn to Palestinians. I was not a great sympathizer with their cause, but why hold the sins of an entire people against one broad? This was not a time for ethnocentric thinking. Nonetheless, when dealing with foreigners of the female persuasion, it's better to be safe than sorry, though it's often more fun to be sorry. I decided

45

I'd have Leila's background checked. It wasn't that I thought she was a spy for the PLO. It was just that some women are sometimes a little more adept than men at wearing masks.

I called Rambam, a friend of mine in Brooklyn who was a private investigator and a couple of other things. Rambam knew the kind of people most folks only watch on the late-night movies. I liked to think of him as a rather militant Jewish Jim Rockford. He was charming and likable, but there were aspects of his life you didn't want to know about. Could land you in a hospital bed.

When I reached Rambam at the offices of Pallorium, his security company, I told him where I was and how I'd got there. 'Interesting,' he said. I told him about the unsavory demise of Rick 'Slick' Goldberg. 'Even more interesting,' he said. I described my meeting Leila and told him she was half Palestinian.

'Forget her,' he said.

I told him Leila and I could be the last hope for peace in the Middle East. It wasn't a bad line, but it was starting to wear about as thin as the Gaza Strip.

'Forget her,' he said.

'Okay,' I said, 'but while I'm busy forgetting her, I'd like you to run a little background check on her.'

'No problem,' said Rambam. There was a certain finality to the way Rambam said 'No problem' that was always comforting to hear. Especially when you thought there was a problem.

I was shaloming off with Rambam when Ratso came careening through the door like a border-town dog. He was obviously excited about something, but if I knew Ratso he was probably going to make me fish for it. I was right.

'Fresh clothes,' he said, putting my New York Rangers hockey bag on the table. 'Probably won't get you into the embassy ball, but they're not as foxed out as whatever you're wearing.'

'They shoot clothes horses, don't they?'

'That's a thought,' said Ratso. 'Hey, maybe the guy with the dart gun was aiming for me.'

'Not likely,' I said.

Ratso shrugged it off. 'Here's your toilet kit,' he said. 'A modern man-about-town can't live without his toilet kit . . .'

'My dear Ratso, I'm eternally grateful to you for bringing my toilet kit, but what is it that you're holding back?'

'. . . Oh yeah, and the cigars. I didn't forget the cigars. But you must promise not to let Big Nurse know that you have them.'

'I'm more worried about the big nerd who's standing here not telling me something I ought to know.'

Ratso feigned injury at my words but he recovered quickly. 'Now really, Sherlock, the doctor says for you to relax and not–'

'My dear Ratso, you're as transparent as a toilet seat cover, though not quite as hygienic. What aren't you telling me? Spit it, goddammit.'

'Well, there were some messages on the machine – one from a broad in Texas – '

'Where in Texas?'

'Texas. I don't know . . . Houston, Austin . . . one of those places.'

'Did you get her name?'

'Yeah. It begins with an L, I think.'

'Linda?'

'No.'

I looked over at the cigars affectionately. 'Lydia?'

'No.'

'Leda?'

'No, it's kind of a Texas sort of name.'

'Bubbette?'

'No. It begins with an *L*. Keep goin'.'

'Lola?'

'No. You really know all these broads?'

'I do very well with women whose names begin with an *L*. I don't know why. All except Lady Luck, of course – she can be a mean-minded, vacuous bitch. . . . Leila?'

'Keep dreamin'.'

'Wait a minute . . . I know who it is. That's great.'

'What's so great about it?' Ratso asked.

'It's the girl in the peach-colored dress,' I said.

'I wouldn't know about that. On an answering machine,' said Ratso, 'all dresses sound gray.'

As it turned out, there'd been one more message on the machine. Ratso described the voice as toneless, flat, and with something almost not human about it. Like death itself, he told me. The voice alone had given Ratso a chill, he said, as he handed me the message he'd transcribed onto a scrap of paper. I didn't have the voice to work with, but the words I read did not radiate warmth to the little hospital corners of my bed. The message read as follows: 'Hey, Kinky. When the cat's away, the mice will play. The next time you sleep, it may be forever.'

'Fred Katz?' Ratso asked, looking over at me.

I read the words again and nodded somberly. 'And I was just starting to like the guy,' I said.

Martin Luther King had a dream; I had a nightmare. It involved Fred Katz, a man I didn't know.

In the dream, Fred Katz's face was weak, fairly handsome, and characterless. He looked like the kind of guy you might see driving a Rolls-Royce around in a small town. But his

48

eyes looked like two angry hummingbirds coming at you beak first. The smile didn't look too healthy either.

He walked over to my hospital bed and spoke to me, but the words were unintelligible. His lips were beginning to look like a flower on Mars. Something even the FTD florist in Fort Worth wouldn't have in stock. Maggotlike tendrils began growing out of his face – not entirely unattractive – and they wriggled like the pale toes of a woman you once loved. He stepped forward quickly with a shiny knife and cut the two green garden snakes in half. Something in mauve from the Dairy Queen began oozing out.

From the corner of my eye I saw him put the knife away and pick up my toilet kit. A deep, biblical-sounding voice, heavy on the echo chamber, boomed out from the sky of the hospital room. It said, 'A modern man-about-town can't live without his toilet kit.'

Katz took the toilet kit and headed for the door. I reached out from the bed to stop him, but suddenly I was tired as hell. Tired of life. Tired of hospitals. Tired of looking at a fact that was as ragged as a death mask.

'Sleep well,' the face said.

Maybe I slept for a few hours. Maybe it was long enough to fall in love, get married, have kids, get divorced, and fight for the custody of a seven-year-old child who looked, laughed, and acted exactly like the spouse you despised. It was only time, and time was just a magazine, and it cost two dollars, and you only had a dollar, and that was life, and life was just a magazine, and who the hell believed what they read anyway?

Eventually, I found myself swimming upward into the rather brackish waters of consciousness. Appropriately, I was doing the American crawl – back from a track-lit, neon nightmare into the pale careless light of the twentieth century. Coffee-colored cobwebs began to clear from my

49

mind. The green garden snakes were back in place. That was nice. What passed for New York sunshine was streaming sluggishly in through the window. But there was something new in the picture.

I didn't know if she was an angel of the morning or a straggler from the *Arabian Nights*, but she was sitting on my bed wearing the naughtiest smile I'd ever seen and not a hell of a lot else.

'Jesus Christ,' I said.

'Try again,' said Leila.

20

There is something very attractive about the prospect of eating, or hosing, forbidden fruit. Leila wasn't exactly forbidden fruit, but she was close enough for color TV. She was wearing a very diaphanous blouse and on her head was a red-and-white sort of scarf that looked like it'd started out in life as a tablecloth in Little Italy.

'I've got two questions for you,' I said, as the smile drilled right through me into the bed where it belonged. 'The first one is, what is that thing you've got on your head?'

The naughty smile turned a bit mischievous, I thought. 'We call it a *kaffiyeh*,' she said. I nodded as if I'd just been told some highly important piece of information. Her breasts filled out the front of the blouse like the humps of a small camel. Not the kind you smoke, but the kind you ride.

'The second question,' I said rather gruffly, after a small pause to study the terrain, 'is, how in hell did you get here?' It's a good policy to keep up a relatively tough-guy exterior. There's always the broad who thinks she's the only one who sees the gentle, sensitive side of you. Whether or not you even have a gentle, sensitive side is pretty much irrel-

50

evant. Women like guys who are hovering at death's door, who've just been shot with a tranquilizer dart, or who've committed some particularly sickening heinous crime that no sane mind on the planet could sanction or absolve. My advice is, if they want to think they see this gentle, sensitive side of you, let them. There'll be plenty of other people in your life who, when you're doing what you believe to be right, will think you're a shmuck.

'Maybe I'm just an ambulance chaser,' she said, 'who's a day late. They wouldn't let me see you yesterday. After I was so curt with you I changed my mind and decided I'd like to get to know you.' She kept studying me. Her eyes were bold and curious.

'C'mere, baby,' I said, 'let me show you where the rabbi bit me.'

She laughed. She may have blushed, but I doubted it. If she did, it got lost in the sunset somewhere west of Mecca. She leaned back on the foot of the bed. The camel rumpled its humps attractively as it crossed the linen desert. Leila had stopped smiling. You could tell she was one of those women who, when they wanted to, had pouting staked out.

Neither of us said a word as she pulled her knees up to her chin and sat on the bed gazing casually through the sheets. She had a beautiful bucket, and I knew damn well that I wasn't the only one who could see that side of her. The construction worker on the ninth floor could see it from the other side of the street.

I thought I'd go for a laugh. Break the implicit sexual tension.

'Speaking of ambulance chasers,' I said, 'my friend Sammy Allred in Austin, Texas, knows a hotshot lawyer who once got a charge of sodomy reduced to following too closely.'

'That sounds nice,' she said.

I might have blushed. If I did, fortunately, it was lost in the implicit sexual tension.

Leila proceeded to explain how, though I'd been rude when she first met me, she'd been strangely drawn to me. Then, as she was taking a break from the cat show, she'd seen the ambulance, and somebody'd told her that I'd been shot. She'd felt terrible. She'd had to see me.

When I asked her for her phone number, she looked at me in an Old World sort of way. Her eyes looked like clear beads on an abacus. Then she smiled, reached into her purse, took out a pink felt marker pen, and looked around either for a piece of paper or to see if anyone was watching.

'Give me your hand,' she said.

I did.

With an almost nasty, jerky little smile, she wrote for a while on the palm of my right hand, then put the pen away, picked up her purse, and stood up to go. My hand felt hot where she'd held it.

'I'll call you when I'm better,' I said.

'No,' she said. 'Call me when you're ready.'

She walked to the door and I looked at my hand. Never be king of the Gypsies, I thought. Couldn't even read my own palm. The writing looked like some kind of blurry, hot-pink hieroglyphics.

'Leila!' I shouted in a commanding, sandpaper voice.

She turned at the door and faced me. Her expression might have been one of fetching mischief. It might have been one of childlike wistfulness. I figured I'd wait until I got the lab report before I decided which. And something told me I might have to wait longer than that. There are some women you can never really get to know until you're dead, and even then you can't be too sure.

'What the hell does this say?' I asked.

'Can't you read it?' she asked playfully. 'It's Arabic numerals.'

21

I remember once reading a newspaper on a sunny veranda on the left coast of our nation. I was having a mimosa cocktail and eggs bend-my-dick and reading an article about what certain prominent Californians planned to do on the Fourth of July. The mayor of Los Angeles was planning to attend a picnic in the park. Cal Worthington, the used-car dealer, was going to lead a parade in Pasadena. But when they asked Henry Miller what he planned to do on the Fourth of July, he said. 'Sleep through it like a bad dream.' That's what I'd planned to do with my Sunday morning. St Vincent's is a long way from St Patrick's.

I would've followed Henry Miller's advice if it hadn't been for McGovern. McGovern, for all his warm and easy-going nature, was positively brutal when it came to smelling a good, unsavory story. I don't know how McGovern got on to me or knew where I was, but it didn't take him long to go for the jugular. He called and wanted to know if the dart gun rumor was true, if it was connected to the murder at the cat show earlier in the week, and if they both were connected to the lost cat I was looking for.

'The hipbone is connected to the assbone,' I said.

'Well, obviously,' said McGovern, 'you're not in the hospital from overwork and exhaustion.' He laughed. 'So the dart gun rumor must be true.'

'Okay,' I said, 'say it is.'

'Now we're getting somewhere,' said McGovern.

'That's what I'm afraid of.' It was bad enough that the cat show was over and most of my suspects were probably scattered to the winds. I didn't need McGovern alerting them further with sensational speculation in the *Daily News*.

'Did you get any response to the lost cat ad?' asked McGovern.

'None of your beeswax, corn bread, or shoe tacks,' I said coolly.

'I can't believe you're saying this. We're in this thing together. MIT . . . MIT . . . MIT . . .' MIT was the name McGovern and I had once given to the 'Man in Trouble Hotline' that we'd established so that if either of us died at home it wouldn't take them eight months to find the body like it did with some guy in Chicago that McGovern had read about. When things got unpleasant, we'd call each other and say, 'MIT, MIT, MIT.'

'McGovern,' I said, 'the problem is that inquiring minds want to know, and if you write about it, inquiring minds may want to hurt Kinky.'

'Okay,' said McGovern, 'this is off the record. Just between us girls. Who was that stone fox who came to see you at the hospital yesterday?'

'Jesus up a Christmas tree, McGovern. What are you doin'? Payin' off the orderlies here?'

'You have your sources; I have my sources,' said McGovern with some little dignity. 'I just heard that this mystery woman visited you in your room and evidently I heard right. They said she was fucking beautiful.'

'McGovern, I've got something for you,' I said. 'It's something you can print.'

'What?'

'Every time you see a beautiful woman, just remember, somebody got tired of her.'

Sunday had three other high points, if you wanted to call them that, besides the call from McGovern. The first one

54

was the lab report. It looked like a doozy, because Robert Young brought it in himself from the eighteenth hole. At least I hoped he'd been playing golf. If not, he was working a string of hookers out of Times Square. Golf is the only opportunity that middle-aged Wasps have to dress up like pimps.

I had been shot, apparently, with an animal tranquilizer named supercalifragilisticexpialidocious. Or something equally as long and tedious.

'Enough to put a lion under,' Robert Young told me and Ratso. 'You can imagine what that would normally do to a man.'

'Kinky the Lion-hearted,' Ratso laughed. I smiled. I was kind of proud of myself in spite of it all. Maybe the years I'd spent abusing my body with drugs on the road had finally paid off – my system was conditioned to it.

'I think you have a very strong will,' said Robert Young.

'I want to live,' I said. 'I want to paint.'

'Nevertheless,' he said, 'I've spoken to Ratso here and he's going to be keeping a close eye on you for the first week. You can go tomorrow, but Ratso will stay with you for a while.'

The idea of my being Ratso's ward was not a pleasant one, but it looked like the only way Robert Young was going to let me out of the hospital. Ratso had moved into the loft with me for a few weeks several years before, when I had been trying to help McGovern out of a hideous snarl he'd gotten himself into. I'd had a little urban hunting accident. Ratso had been dedicated at that time, even devoted. He'd stood up well in the face of death threats, my incapacitation, and harassment from the police. But he was still pretty far down on the list of people on this planet that I'd like to have for a roommate.

To put it kindly, Ratso lacked certain social graces. In fact, he lacked all social graces. And people who lack social graces are the very ones who don't know what you're talking about when you tell them they lack social graces. Anyway, it's not very polite to tell somebody he's a gluttonous, niggardly, unhygienic animal. About all you can say is what a dowdy, humorless woman once told Ratso when he was burping rather loudly in an Indian restaurant: 'Pardon the pig.'

'This could be the end of a beautiful friendship,' I said. 'We've done this before and it was most unpleasant.'

'Well, we're doing it again,' said Ratso.

'Pardon the pig,' I said.

22

It was Sunday night, my last night in the hospital, and Ratso had gone home to pack his Gucci luggage for the big slumber party. Maybe I was being too hard on him, but at least I *knew* I was being an asshole and that meant that I wasn't an asshole.

I'd had a few more visitors by this time. Jane Meara had come by. She was still pining for Rocky and she said what had happened to me was her fault. I said it wasn't her fault. Cooperman came by and asked a few questions. I said I felt like hell and he said he'd see me there. He left. Unfortunately, Leila did not return.

I gazed lovingly at the unsmoked cigars in my toilet kit on the nearby table. There had already been one rather ugly altercation involving myself, the nurse, and the nurse's supervisor over smoking cigars in the hospital room. I argued that cigars smell better than hospitals, but they disagreed. That's what makes for horseracing. In my weakened state, I was hardly a match for them and I lived in fear that they might tell Robert Young and he might keep me at

St Vincent's till the Fourth of July. I decided if I just played my cards right and practiced a certain Gandhi-like abstention, in twelve short hours I would be home smoking like a factory in New Jersey.

I was persevering as best I could when the last call of the day came in. It was Rambam.

'The girl, Leila – the one who's half Palestinian – I checked her out.'

'Great,' I said.

'Not so great,' said Rambam.

'What is she?' I asked. 'Yessir You're-a-Fart's aerobics instructor?'

'The fact that she's half Palestinian is nothing. It's the other half that's the problem.'

'What could be worse?'

'Think about it.'

'Kraut,' I said.

'Worse.'

'Frog.'

'Worse.'

'What could be worse?'

'Try Colombian,' said Rambam. 'She comes from a big, wealthy, powerful Colombian family, with the emphasis on the word *family*. And believe me, they don't get their money growing coffee beans.'

By the time I hung up, I could see the red flag standing up like a small erection in the parking meter of my mind. I didn't know if it meant 'danger' or 'your time is up,' but either possibility seemed sufficiently unpleasant.

I thought of Leila and a chill came over me. It started hot and ended cold. If I knew myself at all, like Ferdinand the Bull, I would probably soon be charging that little flag. And that, on top of everything else, could be very dangerous indeed.

It was a long time before I got to sleep that night. I kept hearing Rambam's last words over and over again: '. . . they don't get their money growing coffee beans . . .'

Where was Robert Young when I needed a cup of Sanka?

23

For a fairly large, cold place, the loft seemed surprisingly cozy. After a stint in the hospital, of course, Houston International Airport would have seemed cozy. But I was glad to be back. And the cat was glad I was back. But the cat was not pleased to see Ratso moving his luggage into the loft.

Cats are a fairly right-wing group politically. They are lovers of the status quo. They don't like anything that might represent change. They hate marriages, divorces, moving days, graduations, bar mitzvahs, bill collectors, rug shampooers, painters, plumbers, electricians, television repairmen, out-call masseuses, Jehovah's Witnesses, and just about everything else, most of which I agree with them about.

Ratso, possibly for the first time in his life, was an agent of change.

The trouble began innocently enough on the first night we were back, with the cat taking a Nixon in one of Ratso's red antique shoes. This is the kind of behavior that, while it may be rather incommoding to the guest, is usually seen as mildly amusing by the cat fancier. It makes the guest feel uncomfortable but it makes the host feel, in a somewhat peculiar, roundabout way, wanted.

'It's just the cat's way of saying "Welcome, Ratso," ' I said, as Ratso threw open the kitchen window to the grim February morning and dumped frozen feline detritus onto the heads of a mother and her two children down on the sidewalk. The sidewalks of New York are famous for many reasons, and one of them is that people have been dumping frozen cat shit onto them for over a hundred years. Pedestrians think it's sleet or some new kind of weather condition. They find it bracing and invigorating.

Ratso's comments will not be recorded here as they do not further the narrative or much of anything else. It is enough to note that they were the kind of ill-humored, unfortunate remarks that one often regrets no sooner than one has uttered them.

By nightfall things were getting back to what passed for normal in New York. Ratso, operating in a rather pioneer mind-set, was under the impression that we might be snowed in for months. Food was his number one priority and I heard him putting in large to-go orders with Joe at Big Wong and with my friend Herb at the Carnegie Deli.

I did not feel that the moment was quite right to tell Ratso we were running low on cat food.

Ratso screened all incoming calls and in general treated me, to my extreme displeasure, like a convalescing maiden aunt.

'You'd make a very good male social secretary, Ratso,' I said. 'Have you ever thought about that line of work?'

'Not really,' said Ratso. He was busy unpacking large books about the life of Jesus as an adolescent and other arcane subjects. Ratso was ignoring my comments and complaints in much the manner that he ignored the presence of the cat. The cat and I were merely two large, troublesome gnats in Ratso's life. For all practical purposes, the cat and I no longer existed. Ratso's domineering manner created a certain resentment in me and I could tell the cat wasn't too keen on it either.

Ratso went to the kitchen and began moving pots and pans and plates around – something the cat disliked intensely – like a predatory insect laying up supplies for the winter. The to-go orders from the Carnegie and Big Wong were due any moment and Ratso was becoming increasingly animated.

He turned to me with a frying pan in his hand and said, 'I'm not just staying here until you're well. I'm staying here until we discover who it was that shot you.'

It was a frustrating but somehow poignant sentiment. I looked at Ratso and shrugged.

'You're going to make somebody a fine homosexual pancake chef,' I said.

The food Ratso had ordered took longer to arrive than you'd think. It always does. The guys at the Carnegie were probably still shaking the matzo ball tree, and the guys from Big Wong were probably still scouring the neighborhood for a small black dog. Matzo ball trees do not fare well in this country, but the small black dog *is* a Chinese delicacy.

Ratso stood by the window staring gloomily into the gloom. In his hands he nervously juggled the little Negro puppet head with the key to the building in its mouth and the brightly colored parachute attached. I sat in the chair by my desk, puffing on a cigar.

'Careful with that,' I said.

'Don't worry,' said Ratso. 'It's the best little head I've had in a while.'

As it happened, both deliverymen arrived at almost precisely the same time. I don't know who was first, but they came up on the same puppet head. With the two delivery guys standing in the doorway, Ratso came over to me and spoke in a voice he thought was a whisper.

'Give me about eighty bucks for the slope food,' he said.

'That's pretty steep,' I said. 'Where's it from – Mr Chow of Beverly Hills?'

'Just give me the cash. . . . Look, I'm pitching in, too. I've got to tip these guys. You'll get something coming back.'

'Sure.'

The truth was that every time Ratso and I had ever split a check, I'd gotten hosed. Then Ratso would always demand the receipt, which he maintained was necessary for his taxes. Once, I tore up the receipt rather than give it to him, and it made Ratso so sad that I vowed never to do it again. So, with the two deliverymen doing an impatient jitterbug in the doorway, I christened Ratso down to sixty-five bucks and let it go.

Ratso tipped the deliverymen, they left, and he started sorting packages all over the kitchen. 'I think,' said Ratso, 'we'll hold the Jew food till the morning and go with the slope food tonight. Or we could mix the two and have sort of a bicultural smorgasbord. Anyway, there's enough here to last us awhile.'

'Wait a minute. How'd you pay for the food from the Carnegie?'

'I worked out a deal with Herb,' Ratso said shiftily.

'What was the deal?'

'He put it on your tab.'

'Good work, Fatso.'

'Don't mention it, Shylock.'

24

At two o'clock in the morning, the cat jumped on Ratso's balls. I'd been waiting for the other shoe to drop, so to speak, and when it happened, I didn't have any trouble recognizing what it was. I didn't see it happen, but hearing a cat jump on somebody's balls is about as down-home an experience as you can have, next to having a cat jump on your own balls.

I leaped sideways out of bed, went into the living room, and saw Ratso holding his testicles and looking around for a weapon. The cat, quite wisely, was nowhere to be seen. So, without the cat, I just had to deal with the Rat.

I had to calm him down first. 'Don't personalize it,' I said. 'It's a territorial situation; it has nothing to do with what the cat thinks of you.' This, of course, was blatantly false, but when a cat jumps on your houseguest's balls you don't rub it in.

'If I find him I'll kill him.'

'It's a female.'

'Might've known.'

'Sanka?'

'Piss off.'

Ratso was understandably upset. He'd given up his bed and his ten thousand books relating to Bob Dylan, Jesus, and Hitler. He'd sacrificed his cable television set, which included forgoing the thing he loved most in life next to food, watching hockey games in a disreputable pair of woolen pajamas. He'd taken a few days off work, moved into a rather strange locus, and possibly put his own life at risk. He'd done all this to help a convalescent country-singer-turned-amateur-detective. And what thanks had he gotten?

But that didn't make things any better for me. I was still weak and subject to periodic dizzy spells. I was trying to locate a killer and a cat before somebody drowned me in a bag. And now I had to cope with a petulant and somewhat torpedolike houseguest.

Being an urban hermit is not the easiest thing in the world to be when you grow up. You feel either crowded or lonely as hell. But at least you feel something. I was feeling like a shot of Jameson.

I walked over to the counter and poured a medicinal

portion into the old bull's horn. Ratso was already back on the couch. I noticed he was sleeping on his stomach.

I downed the shot and thought about Jane Meara, whom I ought to check on. I thought of Fred Katz, whom I ought to find before he found me again. I thought of Sergeant Cooperman, whom I ought to talk to but didn't want to. I thought of Leila, whom I wanted to see. I wasn't better but I was ready. I thought of lots of things, lots of people, lots of reasons why I was me. Maybe someday I'd fall victim to marriage, suburbia, puttering with my lawn, but I couldn't really see it. I'd long ago come to the conclusion that you're born alone, you die alone, and you might as well get used to it. Nothing that Thoreau or Kerouac hadn't already found out, but it was comforting to realize that nothing had changed.

I took another shot and looked over at my boots standing by the desk. They were long and narrow, like my mind. I visualized a person standing in them. Another Kinky, but not like the other Kinkys I'd seen when I first came to in the hospital. It was the Kinky that I could be with a little bit of luck and a hell of a lot of guts. He was a little weather-beaten but he looked all right. You could tell that he didn't have time to be lonely.

There's not that much time left, I thought. There never had been that much time. Never enough to spend the rest of your life looking at the bland face of a child in a yellow station wagon.

The road could've ended anywhere, but it didn't. So you keep driving life's lonely DeSoto, looking ahead into the rain and darkness with the windshield wipers coming down like reaper's blades just missing your dreams. And you don't stop till you're damn well ready. Till you come to the right place. Till you come to the right face. The place may

63

be New York or Texas or it may be somewhere painted with the colors Negroes use in their neon lights.

The face will be smiling. So you take the key out of the ignition and you see if it opens her heart.

25

The phone call from Eugene came at about 6.15 a.m. It was a trifle early and it was also a trifle unpleasant. 'Our little friend,' according to Eugene, had not been idle during the night. Whoever he was, he was continuing his campaign of terror against Jane Meara. Eugene was at Jane's place now because she was frightened to be alone. They wanted to meet me. They had something for me.

I didn't want anything. Maybe another twelve hours of sleep.

I agreed to meet them in an hour at a little Greek coffee shop on Twenty-eighth Street around the corner from Jane's office. I hung up, got dressed, found and fed the cat, and found and lit a cigar. I put on my old hunting vest, my hat, and my coat and I tiptoed across the living room like a guy sneaking out of the house for a poker game. It was my house – I could sneak out of it if I wanted. I locked the door to the loft behind me.

One rule I always follow in life is 'Let sleeping rats lie.'

Vandam Street was windy, cold, and empty in the early morning. There was just a little old lady trying to hold on to a little pink hat and me trying to hold on to my cowboy hat. Deserted as it was, the place had an aura of urban prairie to it. Of course, these days I usually rode two-legged animals.

I drifted up Hudson and hailed a hack. Through the frosty window that wouldn't quite close, I watched the city waken.

A stout woman with a shawl unlocks an iron gate. A man in a woolen cap unloads a crate of oranges from a truck. Down the street another man sits by the gutter next to a whiskey bottle and blows on his hands. Two little children in mackerel-snapper uniforms come out of a building with a doorman. A man wearing a coat walks a dog wearing a sweater.

People walk dogs in Dallas. People walk dogs in California. But in New York sometimes you can see a real man walking a real dog, and there's something timeless and rather beautiful about it. It's performance art.

My mind was starting to wake up a little bit, too. A lot of things were happening to Jane Meara and she wasn't the kind of person things always happened to. She wasn't the kind of person whose junkie boyfriend beat her up or who didn't know that her apartment was being used as a crack kitchen or who found a serial killer in her shredded wheat. She was normal as a blueberry blintze.

So why had somebody kidnapped her cat? Why had somebody left her a crank note at the Roosevelt Hotel? Why had somebody put a bloody butcher knife on her desk? I didn't have any hard answers, but a garish mosaic was coming together in my mind's eyes and it wasn't the kind of thing you'd want to hang in your sitting room.

The cab screeched to a halt at Twenty-eight Street next to a man who was vomiting on a police car. The police car was empty and pretty soon so was the man. Make a nice picture postcard. I paid the driver, got out of the hack, and started walking up the street.

Halfway up the block I found the little Greek coffee shop. It wasn't hard to find the place. You seen one Greek coffee shop, you've seen 'em all. Life imitates John Belushi.

It was a little after seven but the place was already crowded. Eugene and Jane were sitting at a table by the window and waved me over. Jane looked fragile. Eugene looked nervous. The waitress came to the table, Frisbeed a menu at me, and said, 'Whad'll you have?'

I said, 'Coffee.'

She took the menu and went away faster than a dream you weren't sure you had.

'I'm glad you were able to come,' said Jane.

'Let's not get personal,' I said. As a rule, I tried never to appear too sophisticated until the coffee arrived. Jane looked like she was practicing her smile for the first time and Eugene made a let's-get-on-with-the-show gesture.

The waitress brought my coffee. I took a sip and waited. Eugene looked at Jane and Jane looked at Eugene. I looked into my coffee cup and wished I were on a little Greek island instead of in a little Greek coffee shop.

'All right,' I said finally, 'spit it.'

'Well, first of all,' said Eugene, 'there's something I think you ought to know. I didn't tell the police about it the other day for obvious reasons, but I've talked it over with Jane and I think I ought to tell you.'

'Spit it,' I said.

'Well, Jim Landis is my boss. I work with Jane, but he's both of our boss. He's the publisher. He's got his own imprint. You know what that is?'

'I've heard the word.'

'It means he runs his own publishing company.'

'So?'

'So he wasn't in a restaurant like he told the police – he was in Jane's office.' Eugene looked at me nervously. I'd have to check it out but it seemed a bit too easy.

'Maybe I'll order some pie,' I said.

'Landis can't know we talked to you,' said Eugene.

'Autism is my middle name,' I said. 'What else have you got?'

66

Jane reached into her purse, came out with a cassette tape, and handed it across to me. It was an incoming message cassette for an answering machine. 'It's the last message on side B,' she said. 'It came in late last night – about two o'clock in the morning, actually.'

'Okay,' I said. Two o'clock in the morning was about the time the cat had jumped on Ratso's balls. The two incidents were probably unrelated, but it was a time-frame.

'It's a silly message, I know,' said Jane, 'but it scared the hell out of me at the time. In fact, it still does.'

'What was the message?'

'Meow,' said Jane.

'I've heard the word,' I said.

26

By the time I got back to 199B Vandam, it was pushing eight-thirty and Ratso was dunking a bagel into a bowl of wonton soup. The cat was sitting on my desk. Neither of them looked pleased to see me.

The cat knew I was not carrying a grocery bag of cat food. She had a habit of looking in the cupboard with me every time I went to feed her, and she knew we were down to just two cans of Southern Gourmet Dinner. The cat hated Southern Gourmet Dinner.

The cat was merely petulant, but Ratso's expression combined equal components of fury and disgust. I knew he was truly angry when he left his food and began pacing up and down in the kitchen. I was glad I didn't own a rolling pin.

'You are not to go out,' he said with eyes blazing, 'especially these first few days, without first checking with me. Even if you do check with me, I still don't want you going out on the street alone. I'm to know where you're at at all times. Do you understand?'

I took the cassette tape out and put it on the desk. 'Lots of rules for such a small company,' I said.

Ratso continued to stare at me. 'You're goddamn right,' he said.

'Who so hostile?'

'Because you're being an asshole.'

'That's Mr Asshole to you, pal.'

The bickering went back and forth for a while with the cat watching it like a slightly bored tennis fan. I played it out for a few more minutes and then Ratso somewhat grudgingly agreed to listen to the cassette tape with me.

I took the ceramic hat off the top of the large Sherlock Holmes head I kept on my desk and reached inside for a cigar. The Sherlock Holmes head had been given to me by my friends Bill and Betty Hardin at the Smokehouse in Kerrville, Texas. I kept my cigars and other valuables in there. Ratso often said that it was hardly a safe place for valuables, but I always invoked the words of my friend Goat Carson: 'Sooner or later, cats piss on everything.' The way things were going, the cat probably would've pissed on everything by now if it weren't for the little ceramic hat.

I took the tape out of my own answering machine and popped Jane's in. I rewound the tape. Then I pushed the play button. The first voice we heard identified itself as Jim Landis's. It sounded brusque and irritated.

'Jane, it's Jim Landis. . . . It's nine-thirty. . . . What *is* this shit? A monograph on the Flathead Indians of Montana? You think they're happening? You think anybody gives a shit about the Flathead Indians of Montana? I can't believe you sent this on to me – the writing stinks, too – the whole thing sucks. Send the guy to the *National Geographic*. What the fuck's the matter with you, Jane?'

'Pleasant guy to work for,' said Ratso.

'He's got his own imprint,' I said.

'If I worked for him I'd put my imprint on his forehead.'

'Listen.' There was one hang-up and a message from Jane's mother. Then we heard it. It began in a high register and cascaded evilly down to a bone-jarring growl. The same fiendish, half-feline half-human sound we'd heard at the Garden a moment before I'd been shot.

'Any question?' I asked.

'Not a doubt about it,' said Ratso.

I lit my cigar with a rather feeble Bic. I'd had the Bic for four or five days. That was already pretty old in the lifetime of a Bic. I puffed thoughtfully on the cigar.

'I agree,' I said. 'That's our man.'

'Or woman,' said Ratso.

27

'I'm not tailing Hilton Head,' said Ratso as we sat around the kitchen table later that same day. 'I've already spent too much time with that little fruitcake.'

'That's an alarmingly homophobic attitude, Ratso,' I said. I was working on my fifth or sixth espresso and I was starting to get a little buzz.

We haggled back and forth for a while and gradually a division of labor was established. Ratso would, without alerting the parties involved, get a current rundown on Head and the Parks. Head lived in New York, but the Parks had several homes and it wasn't even clear whether they were still in the city.

For my part, I would explore the Fred Katz situation and the 'meow' situation and I would contact Sergeant Cooperman. My investigations were to be conducted telephonically. At least for now, Ratso would do the legwork. It was a reversal of roles that neither of us particularly relished.

It was Tuesday evening, about dusk. In New York in February, of course, it looks like Tuesday evening about dusk most of the time. Ratso was heading for the door with about half of Canal Street on his back. His shoes, pants, shirt, coat, and hat all were exclusively flea-market items. You could say that, in a rather seedy way, he was impeccably dressed. He was a man with deep loyalties to his clothier.

'Don't give up your day job,' I said.

'Don't worry.'

'Just check around a bit. I'd just as soon no one else knows about the dart incident or that we're pressing on with the case.'

'I know what to do.'

Ratso had the door of the loft open when I thought of something else. 'Oh yeah,' I said, 'there's one more thing.'

'What?'

'Would you mind picking up some cat food?'

Ratso closed the door.

Alone in the loft at last, I sat down at my desk and thought things over. If a Gray Line tour had come through 199B Vandam that night, it would've provided a colorful, rather eccentric portrait for the tourists. They would've seen a man sitting alone at a desk in the New York wintertime, smoking a cigar, taking occasional medicinal shots of Jameson from an old black bull's horn, and saying 'meow' repeatedly to himself. But there was no Gray Line tour. Only gray.

The case, as I saw it, was pretty much at a dead end. The cops, according to what I'd read in the papers, had no new leads on the Rick 'Slick' Goldberg murder. In the case of a murdered woman, I'd once read, at least 85 percent of the time the killer is the lover. In the case of a murdered literary agent, the killer could be half the civilized world. Using the word 'civilized' advisedly, of course.

I didn't see what I could do to draw out Fred Katz that hadn't already been done. Maybe skywriting would work. And as for Rocky, well . . .

The slender thread of hope that Jane clung to was probably spurred on by the note, the knife, and the phone message. Maybe Jane thought someone had kidnapped Rocky and was keeping her for ransom or reasons unknown. It was possible, but I doubted it. I'd heard the 'meow' sound twice. Once in person and once on tape. There was something in the nature of the sound itself that made it hard to tell much about the identity of the speaker. There was only one thing that came across loud and clear to me. And that didn't bode well for Jane Meara.

It sounded as if the person didn't like cats.

28

Three cigars and half a bottle of Jameson later, the only thing that really seemed to be clicking was the lesbian dance class. The combination of the Irish whiskey and the residual lion tranquilizer was starting to feel pretty good. It was a rather unorthodox method of mixing drugs and booze, but if everybody did everything the same way it'd be a boring old world.

I was feeling almost numb enough to call Sergeant Cooperman. The game was afoot all right, but with Ratso's new rules in effect it would be impossible, not to say tedious, to try to go anywhere in the next forty-eight hours. Not that there was anywhere to go.

I picked up the blower on the left and dialed the Sixth Precinct.

The desk sergeant sounded tired and frazzled. Tough to be a cop, I thought. But I knew about tough, too, in a different way. Once you've been a country singer on the road for a while, there's not a lot of things in life that you'd think of as tough. Maybe ordering from a wine list.

I gave my name to the desk sergeant, told him I wanted to speak to Sergeant Cooperman, and got put on hold. I'd been there before. In fact, I'd been on hold for some pretty important people in my time. Now I was on hold for a cop.

But on hold was on hold. I knew what to do. I took a few lazy puffs on my cigar and let my imagination fly like an endangered crane. I saw the world through the eyes of Agamemnon, flying into LAX, walking off the plane onto a carpet of blood-red Astroturf. I was Davy Crockett at the Russian Tea Room, fighting off literary agents with my salad fork. A little imagination can be a dangerous thing. You can just have met someone and ten minutes later you're sitting cozily together in a breakfast nook listening to Arthur Godfrey. You can miss a lot of life that way, but it will kill some time when you're on hold.

A gruff, gratingly familiar voice came on the line, bringing me down and back to Vandam Street.

'Well, well,' said Sergeant Cooperman, 'how's Bomba the Jungle Boy?'

'Hangin' in there,' I said.

'The doctor said you were too ill to talk, but much to our joy here at the station house, you seem to've pulled through.'

'Sorry, officer.'

'Maybe you'll do better next time. What do you need, pal?' You can say the word *pal* or you can spit it. Cooperman spit it like slow-moving phlegm from a fast-moving pickup.

'Well, Sergeant, you know I've been looking for this missing cat of Jane Meara's.'

'Yup.'

'And this guy that shot me, just before he shot me, he said the same thing someone left on Jane Meara's answering machine last night. I was wondering if we couldn't make a voiceprint or voice comparison of some kind and – '

'It's inadmissible. What's the phrase?'

'What?'

'What's the *phrase*?'

'Well, it's just a word, actually.'

'Impossible. What's the word?'

'Meow.'

There was a long silence on the line. It was so long that I thought maybe he'd gone out to answer a ten-four or something. Finally, he spoke.

'Bow-wow,' he said.

'You don't have to bark at me.'

He hung up.

29

It was 11.30 p.m. Ratso was still not back and the cat was not in a very talkative mood, so I picked up the blower on the left and dialed a number I'd recently conjugated from my right hand.

'Hello,' came a sleepy voice.

'Shit,' I said. 'Are you asleep?'

'Kinky?'

'How'd you know?'

'I could smell your cigar,' she said dreamily.

'Leila – you really like the way my cigars smell?' It was too good to be true.

'I love it.' What a wonderful girl.

One thing about cigars is they save a lot of time with broads. If you find a girl who likes your cigar smoke, it usually means she likes a lot of other things, too. And most of the time, but not always, it means you've got her in your hip pocket. Either she's the kind of broad who loves not to like it, or she's unconsciously trying to get closer to her grandfather who smoked cigars and was run over by a trolley when she was six years old.

In either case, forget the Freudian implications, which is always good advice. What you're left with is a wholesome, earthy, soulful, open-minded, old-fashioned, sensuous person of the female persuasion.

It also means you can smoke your pie and eat it, too.

When I hung up, Leila and I had agreed to get together at eight the following night at her place, which was fairly close by in the Village. She gave me the address.

I put on my Borneo sarong from Peace Corps days, killed the light, and got into bed. I'd given up waiting for Ratso and I wasn't worried about how I was going to slip out of the loft the following evening.

I was just thinking about a certain Middle East hot spot that, with a little bit of shuttle diplomacy, was soon going to explode.

30

I did not dream of Leila that night. I dreamed of androgynous-looking cats doing a form of St. Vitus's ballet around my bed. Many times during the night I willed them to go away. Jump on Ratso's balls or something. Wherever he was.

The cats would disappear for a while, but then they'd return, doing poisonous little pirouettes in ever-tightening circles inside my brain. They all wore masks, of course. And hideous Day-Glo leotards. They were supple and sinuous – sexy in a feline sort of way. The little bastards were macho about being androgynous.

When the dancing cats had finally buggered off into the darkness, it was almost dawn and the garbage trucks were beginning to gnash their teeth outside my window. I was tired as hell but I couldn't sleep. All I could seem to do was think. And what I was thinking was not very pleasant.

By dawn's surly light I was all but convinced that the androgynous dancing cats had been trying to tell me something. They were trying to tell me that all of this fit together somehow. It seemed as easy as connecting the dots that were dancing before my bloodshot eyes.

There was no room for coincidence now. The man who called himself Fred Katz was a very sick puppy. He'd left the 'cat got you tongue' note at the Roosevelt and he'd killed Goldberg and gotten *his* tongue. I felt certain it was he who was behind the series of pranks that had occurred – the knife, the phone message. Fred Katz had also, I believed, tried to kill me.

Find Fred Katz, I thought, and you'd have the cat and the killer. The more I thought about it, the more desperate and deadly the situation seemed.

I wasn't worried about what was going to happen to Rocky anymore. But I was worried – very deeply worried – about what was going to happen to Jane Meara.

31

It took me longer than the prime of Miss Jean Brodie to find Leila's street. I didn't mind the little walking tour of the Village, though. It was a clear night and cold as hell. 'Bracing,' as they say. It doesn't matter how horrifically cold it gets in the city, New Yorkers always think it's bracing. That's one of the reasons New York isn't Buffalo. In Buffalo, they think it's cold.

I was just thankful to be out of the loft where there was nothing to do but stroke the cat and Ratso's rapidly developing ego. He seemed to be overidentifying with his

Dr Watson role. That morning we'd killed the remaining wonton soup and knocked down about seven espressos at a breakfast power caucus.

Ratso's appetite for the case had increased dramatically. It was just over a week ago that I'd had to drag him by the heels to the Garden to help me find a missing cat. Now he couldn't wait to get back on the track of the mysterious Parks and Hilton 'Fruitcake' Head. Amateur detectives are hard to figure.

The other thing that had been irritating about Ratso at the power caucus was how close to the vest he'd played his cards. It was an 'ongoing investigation,' he'd said. He'd 'fill me in when he knew more.' Almost like talking to Sergeant Cooperman.

The good thing about Ratso's active involvement in the case, however, was that I had no trouble slipping out to meet Leila. I didn't even feel too guilty about breaking the house rules. Besides, I was starting to feel better. It only hurt when I meowed.

By the time I found Leila's street the numbing cold had put Jane Meara's situation out of my mind. I lit a cigar with a new pastel-purple Bic I'd bought from a rather hostile Pakistani at a corner grocery store. Now I was looking for street numbers and trying not to freeze my *huevos* off. Three more blocks and I stumbled on the place.

Leila lived in a fairly modern building named after a French painter who'd once been fairly modern himself. That was over a hundred years ago and now he was dead and famous enough to have a wino urinating on a building named after him. A nice touch, if you belonged to the Impressionist school.

I walked into a small lobby with a large doorman. He planted himself directly in my path.

'Can I help you?' he asked. His eyes looked like little locked glass doors.

'Twelve-K,' I said.

'Name of the person you wish to see?' he asked, looking at my hat.

'Leila.'

'And your name is – ?'

'Kinky.'

He went to the house phone, dialed a couple numbers, and said, 'Mr Kinky is here.'

He listened, nodded, put down the phone, and motioned me in. I bootlegged my cigar into the elevator and pushed twelve. I stood back to enjoy the ride. Took a few puffs on the cigar. Thought neutral elevator thoughts.

I took a left on twelve, found 12K at the end of the hall, and knocked on the door. After a moment the door opened. It wasn't Leila. It was a stockily built, swarthy man with a large mustache. Looked like an organ grinder who'd just stomped his monkey to death.

'Come in,' he said.

32

I peered around Jerry Colonna and saw a red sparkle-topped tennis shoe resting casually on a glass coffee table. A bare Arabian ankle was growing luxuriantly out of the tennis shoe like the stalk of a sexy tropical plant. I'd have to look it up in *National Geographic* sometime and find out if it was a man-eater. The guy backed up a little and I stepped into the room.

The place looked like a whorehouse in *Architectural Digest*. There was a lot of glass, a lot of metal, mirrors everywhere, and a forty-foot couch done up entirely in bullfight-poster red.

'Understated,' I said to the man with the mustache.

He didn't say anything. His eyes looked hot and distant. Staring at his face was like flying over a forest fire in the middle of the night at thirty-seven thousand feet. You knew it couldn't burn you, but you also knew that one of these days they were going to have to land the plane.

'It's okay, Hector,' said a familiar feminine voice. The guy stepped to the side and I saw that the bare ankle was attached to an equally bare, slightly thin, sinuously gorgeous leg. Leila was attached to the leg.

'Kinky's harmless,' she said with a smile. She was wearing a pair of faded, delicious-looking cutoffs and a tight pink T-shirt that said something in one of the Romance languages. I gave her a harmless wink.

I walked a little closer to the couch. 'What's a Hector?' I said.

She gave a little papal sign with her right hand and Hector nodded once and left the room. 'Hector works for my brother,' Leila said.

'Maybe your brother's taking being an equal opportunity employer a step too far.'

She smiled a top-drawer mischievous smile, crooked her finger, and beckoned me around the coffee table.

'Maybe I've got a job for you,' she said.

'Like what?' I asked as I sat down next to her.

'I don't know,' said Leila, 'but you'd look pretty cute handing me a dry towel.'

You might say that a forty-foot-long couch isn't very cozy and you'd be right. But given a spiritually horny American and a rather randy Palestinian, it can be just about everything else.

Leila had turned the lights down to low interrogation. She had turned me on to the point where I was one step away from making water wings out of her cutoffs. We were both trying to chew the same piece of Dentyne when a slender, vaguely sinister figure appeared in the hall doorway. When the lights came up we hardly noticed. Dentyne can be a very sexy gum.

Leila recovered first. 'Kinky,' she said, '... this is my brother, Carlos.'

'Carlos?' I said. I sat up. It was a chore to get my breath back.

'Carlos,' said Carlos. His expression hadn't changed since I'd first seen him standing there. His face looked like a sweet, evil puppet that enjoyed pulling all the strings itself. I didn't know if Colombians liked guys practically hosing their sisters on forty-foot couches but I doubted it, so I tried to leaven the situation.

'Carlos,' I said. 'Carlos ... wait a minute ... not Carlos the international terrorist?'

His eyes took on the unmistakable glint of primitive obsidian tools used to bring death to small animals. A rather unpleasant hissing noise came from Carlos's mouth. Then he was gone.

'I don't think he considers me a prospective brother-in-law,' I said.

'He'll get over it,' said Leila. 'Wait right here.'

I waited. Leila got up and walked out of the room into the hallway. Nice bucket, all right. I heard a door open and close. I took out a cigar and lit it and looked at a picture of the sad, lonely face of a bull in the ring. I didn't like Spanish-speaking peoples because they were mean to bulls. Of course, maybe if the Krauts, Turks, and Communists had had some bulls around they would've left the Jews, Gypsies, Armenians, Cambodians, and everybody else alone. I puffed on the cigar and watched the reflections of smoke disappearing in one of the mirrors across the room. Life is but a dream.

I waited. You'd think Hector would've come in and asked me if I'd like a nice cup of Colombian coffee. I waited.

The next time I looked up I saw a vision coming toward me in a light-pink afghan coat with a red-and-black-checked Italian tablecloth on its head.

'Nice gefilte,' I said.

'Kaffiyeh,' said Leila.

She put a rectangular cloth bag on the glass tabletop. It looked like a Gucci shoeshine kit. She opened it and began taking out some of the most ornate drug paraphernalia I'd seen this side of the East Village. A two-pronged silver coke spoon in the form of a sacrificial maiden with arms outstretched. A large seashell container with a mirror on one side and an inch of what looked like diplomatic-pouch-quality snow on the other. Finally, she took one end of a tubelike device that branched into two silver globes and handed it to me. The other end remained in the Gucci shoeshine kit.

'This is for you, Kinkster. Do you know what it is?'

'Looks like a stethoscope for a pinhead.'

Unfortunately, I did not need a great deal of coaxing. I put one silver globe against each nostril, inhaled sharply, and simultaneously blew my brains out.

It was so good it was very dangerous. Just like all the other good things in life.

33

I don't remember how I got out of that room. Maybe I flew by Jewish radar. Maybe the faces of John Belushi and Lowell George guided me like Sherlock Holmes carriage lamps shining through the mist. Whatever it was that got me there, I was glad to be outside.

It was America. It was 1988. I didn't know it, of course. The right lobe of my brain was just beginning to recouple with the left lobe. I could feel the clumsy, gloved hands of Russian cosmonauts slowly piecing the machinery together somewhere in space.

I could hear Leila's voice, soft and intimate, somewhere next to me. Cocaine always sends men and women to different planets. 'I could go for a man who doesn't wear running shoes,' she said.

I did a few impromptu deep-breathing exercises and looked around to get my bearings. Incredibly, we were still on Leila's block, just a few houses down from where she lived. It was hard to believe that I'd felt brain-dead for what seemed like an eternity. How could I have almost allowed my childhood dreams, my dearest hopes for the future, my very existence on this planet to be reduced to a mere fossil record on the dusty, forgotten desk of some mildly interested, science-oriented graduate student who'd gone out for a pizza without anchovies?

The wind began to blow a little harder and a lot colder. I began to notice a few things. Two of them were Leila's legs. As the wind whipped up her coat I saw she was still wearing the cutoffs underneath. Her legs looked as pink as the house where The Band used to practice with Bob Dylan.

'Your legs look cold,' I said. I took her hand and we walked a little farther. She didn't say anything.

'Maybe I could blow on them,' I said.

'Maybe.'

We were each lost in our own thoughts on our own different planets when we came face to face with Sergeant Mort Cooperman and Sergeant Buddy Fox. They appeared to be in a hurry.

81

'One side, Tex,' said Cooperman brusquely. Fox looked appreciatively at Leila, we both stepped aside, and they continued at a brisk pace up the sidewalk.

Standing in the gutter I turned and saw cops getting out of several unmarked cars and heading in the same direction as Cooperman and Fox. Four of them were carrying a long metal pole with a sort of phallic knob on the end of it. There were two handles on each side. It was a battering ram.

They all went to Leila's building and they didn't seem to be having any trouble with the doorman. I took Leila's arm and hurried her farther down the street and around the corner.

'What do you think's happening?' she asked a little too coolly.

'I don't know,' I said. 'Maybe somebody tore the tag off their mattress.'

34

Thursday morning broke cold, grim, and gray in New York. My hangover and I stepped gingerly around the cat litter box, which was blocking the doorway to the bathroom. I usually kept the cat litter box in the shower, except, of course, when I was taking a shower. The reason for the cat litter box displacement soon became evident.

Ratso was taking his biannual shower. It was a sort of a purification rite with Ratso and he followed it almost religiously whether he felt he needed it or not.

And he was singing.

Because of my years on the road as a country singer, I had come to hate the sound of the human voice singing. To make matters worse, Ratso was singing some half-punk, half-rap song by his favorite new group, Smoking/No Smoking. Unfortunately, or perhaps fortunately, depending on how you looked at it, both the song and the band would be passeκ before Ratso stepped out of the rainroom, a visual experience I did not wish to have at that hour of the morning.

I went to the sink, wiped some steam away from the mirror, and saw that my hair was standing straight up in the shape of a rocket ship. It was a fairly current New York hairstyle but it didn't blow my skirt up too much. I got a brush and ran it through my moss a few times, brushed my choppers, drew a bye on shaving. My eyes wouldn't've looked good in a stuffed rabbit's head.

Ratso showed no signs of departing the rainroom, so I opted for a little trick I'd picked up on the road. It was known widely in country music as the Waylon Jennings Bus Shower. You stand close to a sink and splash water on your face and your armpits. If there's soap around you can use it, but then you have to splash a lot of water on your armpits to get it off.

There was soap and I used it. The results left my sarong and the bathroom floor pretty wet, but when you thought about it, it was a small price to pay for being well groomed.

I went back into the kitchen and looked out the window at the bleak warehouse walls and rusty fire escapes across Vandam Street. The hangover was starting to go, but I still didn't feel like pulling hotcakes on the griddle and taking down the ol' fiddle.

I stoked up the espresso machine and fed the cat.

While I waited for the espresso I paced back and forth and thought about what had transpired on the previous night. It was the kind of situation where you hated yourself in the morning but you were still pretty damn glad that you'd done it.

Before I knew it the espresso was ready.

I poured a cup, lit my first cigar of the morning, and sat

down at the kitchen table to read Ratso's copy of the *Daily News*. On page 2 I saw a headline that almost made the espresso come out my nose. It read:

MAJOR COKE RING BUSTED
Country Singer Thought to Be Finger

35

'Great follow-up,' said Ratso from over my shoulder. He was wearing some kind of New Wave bathrobe that hurt my eyes. I turned my attention back to the story.

'Terrific sequel,' he said.

'What the hell are you talking about?'

'Terrific sequel,' he said, 'to "Country Singer Plucks Victim from Mugger." ' At this point Ratso leaned over and began to read the story aloud.

'Let's see,' he said. ' "Although law enforcement offices refused to comment, an informed source revealed that a well-known country singer was seen leaving the premises just prior to the time of the raid. The Texas singer, who has often performed at the Lone Star Cafe, is known to have been involved with crime-solving on an amateur level in the past. . . ." ' Ratso stood up straight and put his hands on my shoulders.

'What you need is an agent, Kinkster,' he said excitedly. 'What you need is a manager.'

'What you need is a muzzle for Christmas,' I said.

Ratso looked hurt. He stood beside the kitchen table like a large, wounded sparrow. I didn't let it get to me.

Ratso had carefully cultivated that hurt look and he was pretty damn good at it. When I was hurt, I only looked confused, nervous, or angry. So a hurt look wasn't a bad thing to have. Could keep you from getting hurt sometime.

'You see, my dear Ratso,' I said, 'there was only one mugger. Surely you realize there must be thousands of Colombians in New York whose mustaches intersect in the illegal drug trade.'

Ratso thought about it for a moment. So did I. The cat jumped up on the windowsill and watched a few toxic snowflakes crash-land on the East Side, far corner of the pane.

'You don't really think,' said Ratso, 'that they'd put all of this together and come looking for us, do you?'

I got up from the table, poured another shot of espresso into my Imus in the Morning coffee mug, and watched the cat watch the snow.

'As Albert Einstein used to say, Ratso, "I don't know." '

As the snow drifted down, our conversation drifted to other matters. I was midway into my second cigar and finishing my third espresso when Ratso unburdened himself of the results of his adventures in the past few days as an amateur detective. I listened politely.

To hear Ratso tell it, he'd run a very thorough-going investigation into the three parties in question. Unfortunately, I hadn't thought about them in so long that they seemed like characters in an old Russian folk story. It was beginning to dawn on me that, even for an amateur, I had not been very professional. I had let Marilyn and Stanley Park and Hilton Head, as well as the better part of caution and common sense, be pushed to the back of my mind by Leila's beautiful legs.

'. . . and so Stanley Park's been missing in action for almost a week,' Ratso was saying. 'Nobody's seen him, and get this . . .'

'Don't talk while you're eating.'

'. . . Head may not be as much of a winkie as we at first thought,' Ratso continued.

'I'll take that dry towel now.'

'. . . at least three occasions coming out of Marilyn Park's building . . .'

'Yes, you can borrow my toothbrush, but in some cultures it means we're engaged.'

'. . . and on a fourth occasion – are you listening, Kinkster? – coming out of his own place with . . .'

'Leila!'

'That's right. Hilton Head was coming out of his own place with Leila. How'd you know that?'

'Call it cowboy intuition,' I said. 'She was too good to be true.'

It figured.

36

As Archie Goodwin, Nero Wolfe's famous sidekick, once observed, 'No man was ever taken to hell by a woman unless he already had a ticket in his pocket, or at least had been fooling around with timetables.'

I hadn't been taken to hell yet, but I could sure see it coming. A lot of things were going on and I didn't like any of them. If I was going to solve this case and live to hear Ratso take credit for it, I'd better be damn careful and lucky. Of course, if I'd really been lucky I'd've been in a park somewhere in Oregon throwing a Frisbee to a dog with a bandanna around its neck and I never would've gotten Jane Meara's phone call in the first place. Of course, then I never would've met Leila.

Around eleven Ratso went out for a while to check on things at his apartment. When you've got a stuffed polar bear's head, a four-foot-tall statue of the Virgin Mary, ten thousand books relating to Jesus, Bob Dylan, and Hitler, and a couch with skid marks on it, you can't just run off and leave things.

After Ratso had departed I hopped off the espresso and poured a stiff shot of Jameson into the bull's horn. I toasted the cat rather briefly and killed the shot. I called Leila's old number and got a recorded message saying that it had been disconnected.

I called Rambam. He wasn't home, so I left a message for his machine to call my machine and maybe the two machines could get together and have lunch at the Four Seasons. I also mentioned for Rambam to be sure to read page 2 of the *Daily News* and let me know what he thought about it.

The more I thought about it myself, the less likely I believed it was that members of a major Colombian cocaine cartel, as the *Daily News* described the operation, would take the time and effort to identify one country-singer-turned-amateur-detective. It seemed to me, as I sat in the loft that Thursday afternoon and knocked back another shot of Jameson, that it was even less likely that they would take any action. They had plenty of bulls to fight, and if they ran out of bulls there was always each other.

As the morning wore on, I started to feel a bit more secure about the whole thing. I just wouldn't throw the puppet head down to anybody wearing a big mustache.

About noon I opened the refrigerator and was able to locate a residual bagel behind a small city of Chinese take-out cartons, some of them dating back to before the Ming Dynasty. The bagel was in surprisingly good shape. In fact, it felt better than I did.

I took the bagel and a bottle of Dr Brown's black cherry soda over to the desk, and with the cat, two telephones, and an old typewriter, I had lunch. Fairly pleasant dinner companions, as they go.

After lunch I opened the day's correspondence with my Smith & Wesson knife. There wasn't a hell of a lot to open. If you want a pen pal, you've got to be a pen pal.

There was something that looked unpleasantly like a wedding invitation. I slit it open and sure enough it was. A girl I used to know named Nina Kong was getting married. In order to do this she must have straightened out her act in more ways than one. The guy she was marrying was Edward S. Pincus, a rising young urologist. The wedding was at the Pierre Hotel. Reception to follow.

Apparently the happy event had taken place two days ago. You know the mails.

I started to throw the invitation out and then thought better of it. Placed flat on the desk, it made a pretty fair coaster for the Dr Brown's black cherry soda.

A house isn't really a home without a coaster. I gave the cat a crooked smile. The cat smiled back.

It was downhill from there. A form letter from a Catholic priest in Nicaragua, which had come addressed to 'Occupant.' A bill from Con Ed. A letter from a militant lesbian coalition called Sisters of Sappho, which I inadvertently opened before I realized it was for Winnie Katz.

Bringing up the tail end of the day's correspondence was a postcard from the Pilgrim Psychiatric Center. It was from my old friend Cleve, the former manager of the Lone Star Cafe. It read as follows: 'Don't believe the doctors. There's nothing lamp carrot rocking-horse wrong with me. Wish you were here.'

That was the lot. One of these days I'll reverse my zip code and see what happens.

I called McGovern at the *Daily News* and he vehemently denied having anything to do with the story on page 2. He asked me if I'd been at the scene of the bust. I vehemently denied having anything to do with it. We both vehemently hung up.

I got a screwdriver and turned the old black-and-white television set that was missing a knob on to *Wild Kingdom*. I moved to Ratso's couch and the cat moved to her rocking chair. I lay down for a little power nap, and an idea gradually began forming in the back of my mind amidst all the debris that Leila's legs had recently kicked there. The idea rose like a phoenix, no doubt from the ashes of several rather charred brain cells. It started off a little shaky, but it looked like it was going to fly.

I did not especially like *Wild Kingdom*. I always felt that the feeling was Mutual of Omaha. The cat, however, always seemed vaguely to enjoy the show, so I turned it on every now and then for her enjoyment.

It wasn't a great sacrifice for me. Just part of the give-and-take of daily life. A little adjustment we make in order to ensure that the world becomes a better place for our children and our kittens. On the other hand, it could've been that, subconsciously, these little kindnesses I performed were a trick I was playing on God to make Him think I was a more sensitive American than I am. But could any man play a trick on God? Whose *Wild Kingdom* was it anyway? Was it God's or Mutual of Omaha's? Tune in next week.

Ratso walked in just about the time I got the phone call from Sergeant Cooperman.

37

After I'd established that Ratso was not going to interrupt his journey to the refrigerator to answer the phones, I walked over to the desk and collared the blower on the left.

'Start talkin',' I said.

'Goodbye, Tex,' said Sergeant Cooperman.

'Going somewhere, Sergeant?'

'Yeah. Funeral of a guy. Used to be a country singer. Tried his hand at a little amateur crime-solving now and then. Got lucky a few times. Then he got in over his head. Colorful character, he was. Gutsy guy, too. Never liked him too much, personally. . . . Never got off on funerals much, either. I'll take a fucking wake any day.'

'I know what you mean. I'd rather go to an Irish wake than a Jewish wedding. They're more fun.'

Ratso looked over at me inquiringly from the refrigerator. I shrugged and took a fresh cigar out of Sherlock Holmes's head.

'Got a mick in the woodpile somewhere, do you, Tex?' While I listened to Cooperman chuckle I began preignition procedures on the cigar. For a while I thought he had the chuckle on an endless loop, but it subsided neatly right about the time I had the cigar ready for lift-off.

'Gonna wear a Colombian necktie to the funeral, Tex?'

'I must assume, then,' I said, 'that this call's in reference to "Country Singer Thought to Be Finger." ' I took a not-so-relaxed puff on the cigar.

'Let me tell you something you obviously don't know,' said Cooperman. 'These guys don't operate like the Mafia. They don't make a precise, targeted hit. It ain't like the Tongs either, where they let the honky customers continue eating their sweet-and-sour pork while they blow away the enemy slopes at the next table. These are the kind of guys that like to waste the grandmother in the wheelchair, the dog, the cat. They see a two-month-old baby in a crib, they ice it. And believe me, they don't pick the rattle up off the floor. If they come for you, every bag lady and hot-dog vendor on Vandam Street will go with you. You're not dealing with Ricardo Montalban here.'

The chuckle was gone from Cooperman's voice. Even the malice was gone. Things were worse than I'd thought. I needed a drink.

'You know,' Cooperman continued almost wistfully, 'when I think of two Jewish meatballs like you and your pal Ratso trying to stay ten steps ahead of a private army of bloodthirsty spics with an intelligence network that's probably superior to the FBI . . .'

Cooperman sighed. I tried to swallow. Sometimes it's harder than it looks.

'You might have been set up, pal,' he said. 'Or maybe somebody's using you for a tethered goat. I can't prove it. In fact, if anybody asks, I didn't even say it.'

'Maybe you're wrong,' I said. 'Maybe they won't figure it out. Maybe they won't bother to come after us.'

'Maybe I'm a nigger jet pilot,' said Cooperman.

I put my cigar down in the middle of a big, Texas-shaped ashtray. It looked lonely there, burning away deep in the heart of Texas. I hardly noticed Ratso, who, by this time, was hovering close to the desk like an expectant father.

'Well,' I said, 'other than renting a stateroom on the *Titanic*, what do you suggest we do?'

'Absolutely nothing. And keep your fingers crossed. I got to run.'

'One more thing,' I said. 'What's a Colombian necktie?'

'That,' said Cooperman, 'is where they slit your throat vertically, pull your tongue out through the opening, and let it hang down your neck. Colombian necktie.'

'Nah, don't think I want it. Too trendy. It'd clash with my hunting vest.'

'Wear whatever you want,' said Cooperman. 'It's your funeral.'

38

When I finally got to sleep that night, I dreamed I was in the office of a beautiful female psychiatrist. Apparently things hadn't been working out too well for me and I was seeing this lady shrink to find out what was wrong.

'Have you ever been involved in joshman?' she asked. She lowered her voice slightly when she said the word *joshman*.

'What is joshman?' I asked.

She seemed a little surprised that I didn't know. She looked at me for a moment. Then she said very clearly and distinctly, 'Joshman is when a man kisses another man on the knees.'

I woke up suddenly. I'd heard a sound that I didn't think belonged in the dream. I hit the lights and checked the clock by my bedside. Closing in on 3 a.m. I listened.

Except for Ratso's rather unpleasant snoring, there was nothing. I was almost ready to kill the light and get back to my joshman dream when I heard it again. Sounded like a muffled clang. Maybe it was a shy trolley. I walked over to the bedroom window and looked, but it didn't do much good. No one had opened that window or even seen through it in forty-seven years. Not that there was much of a view. Garbage-truck docking area.

Grime was a nice word for what was covering the outside of the window. It was rusted shut tighter than some people's minds. The window worked about as well as everything else in the loft. I kind of liked it that way. Always live in a house that's older than you are.

I heard the sound again. This time I had it. A drunk throwing rocks against the fire escape. It was as common in New York as crickets in the country. Then a shrill voice that sounded like it was coming all the way from Brooklyn shattered the night.

'Hey, Tom fucking Sawyer! Throw down the goddamn puppet head!'

It was Rambam.

I walked across the cold floor of the loft, past Ratso's torporous body, past the cat stirring slightly in the rocker, to the kitchen. I turned the kitchen light on. If the Colombians wanted me, I figured they could dream up more creative methods than shooting a man standing at a window.

The puppet head smiled down on me from on top of the refrigerator. The puppet head always looked like it was smiling. You'd look like you were smiling, too, if you had a large house key wedged in your teeth.

I picked up the puppet head, opened the window, and read Vandam Street like a gutsy quarterback who was playing hurt. Rambam came out of the darkness from my right at a measured pace. Throwing into the wind, I tried to lead him, but the parachute didn't hang quite as much as I'd expected. He had to run into the gutter and halfway onto the street to make the catch.

'Complete to Rambam,' he shouted.

I closed the window before I froze to death. Through the window, I watched Rambam with no little degree of fascination as he spiked the puppet head in the gutter.

Rambam came in the door wearing his green Israeli Army jacket just about the time I was getting into my old hunting vest. East meets West. Or, if you spoke with a Yiddish accent, East meets vest. It wasn't terribly funny. It was just the kind of thing you think of when you don't want to think about everything else.

'Parked way up the street,' said Rambam, as he flipped

me the puppet head. 'In case the Colombians try to put a potato in my tailpipe.'

I examined the puppet head carefully. It looked happier, more alive, and more purposeful than many faces I passed on the street every day. And it didn't use the word *marvelous* too much. I was starting to get kind of attached to it. I placed it gently back on top of the refrigerator.

'Alas, poor Yorick,' I said, 'you have a head the size of a LeSueur pea.'

I took the bottle of Jameson and two appropriately stemmed glasses and sat down at the desk with Rambam. We had a round or two and I ran down for him everything that had happened in the last twenty-four hours. Leila's apartment, Leila, Hector, Carlos, meeting Cooperman and Fox on the street before the bust, the *Daily News* story, and Cooperman's phone call earlier in the evening. The only thing I didn't tell him about was the joshman dream. I didn't think it was pertinent to the case. Also, I didn't want any spurious rumors flying around New York about unfounded joshman episodes in my past. Even one can ruin a guy.

When I'd finished telling Rambam everything I knew about the Colombians, which wasn't a hell of a lot, he sat back in the chair and thought about it for a moment. Then he took the bottle and poured us both another shot.

'You're leaving tomorrow,' he said. 'You and Ratso. You're going back to your ranch in Texas and you're going to stay there. I'll pick you up and put you on a plane. All you got to do is pack, check the plane schedules, and call me and I'll pick you up. Any problem with that?'

'Well,' I said.

'Fine. That's it.' He stood up. 'Look,' said Rambam, 'the average detective, third grade, earns about thirty-six thousand a year. The average Carlos character spends more than that a *day* just on payoffs. They know all about you already. You've got zero chance. I'll pick you guys up tomorrow.'

'You want to crash here?'

'Where the hell am I gonna sleep?'

'Well,' I said, 'you could sleep on the couch with Ratso.'

'Or?'

'Or you could sleep in the bedroom with me. There's only one bed, but we could put a guitar case between us like we used to do on the road with the band to keep us from accidentally hosing somebody in the middle of the night.'

'Thanks for the offer,' said Rambam. 'It's very attractive, but I don't want to wake up with a Colombian butterfly.'

'What's a Colombian butterfly?' I asked.

'That's where they take your lungs out of you while you're still alive, and leave them suspended outside your body.'

'Charming,' I said.

'Sweet dreams,' said Rambam.

After he'd left I walked over to the kitchen window and looked out into the nothingness of the New York night. It almost didn't matter whether all this stuff was real or not. It was bad enough either way. I didn't know what to think. I didn't know what to do.

I stared into the darkness again and I thought of Wyatt Earp's brother Virgil's last words. All of the Earp brothers were very close and they were said to have believed strongly in life after death. The legend is that when Virgil was dying after a gunfight, Wyatt knelt by his brother's side in the dust and asked him what he saw.

'Wyatt,' he reportedly said, 'I don't see a fuckin' thing.'

39

New York's a tar baby. Once you're here, it's hell to get away. Like most New Yorkers who plan to leave the city, we didn't make it.

Everyone thinks they're not going to die in New York. Everyone thinks they're going to die someplace nice like St Penisburg, Florida. Everyone is wrong.

There are some interesting, if not particularly relevant, exceptions. Of course, when the subject is death it's sometimes hard to say what might or might not be relevant. Maybe nothing's relevant. Be that as it may, Damon Runyon – born, of course, in Manhattan, Kansas – wanted to die in New York and did, and had his ashes scattered over Broadway from a small plane flown by Eddie Rickenbacker. George S. Kaufman, the playwright, wished to die in New York and he also got his wish. Kaufman, however, requested in his will that his ashes be thrown in the face of the theater critic for *The New York Times*.

The only other guy that ever did anything very significant with his ashes was Joe Hill, who was wrongfully tried and hanged on a trumped-up charge in Utah. Joe Hill's ashes were scattered, at his request, in every state of the union except Utah. Never cared for Utah much myself.

The lesson in all of this, I suppose, is that it's a good thing to get your ashes hauled as much as possible before they're finally scattered.

Ratso was waking up.

It was not a nice thing to see.

I busied myself with feeding the cat some tuna and the espresso machine some ground coffee beans while Ratso proceeded with his morning ablutions. By nine o'clock Friday morning, Ratso and I were drinking cups of espresso and looking at each other across the kitchen table like Ward and June Cleaver.

I filled Ratso in on Rambam's visit and told him what Rambam had advised. He seemed to take it soberly enough.

'We've been warned twice now,' I said. 'Once by Cooperman and once by Rambam. Of course, you don't have to stay here in the loft or go to Texas. You could leave now and go to your place or lie low somewhere else.'

'Yeah,' said Ratso, 'but if their intelligence network is superior to the fucking FBI, they already know more about me than my mother. I think we're in this one together, Kinkster. And I don't really believe these guys are going to come after us. Anyway, it's too late to run and they don't have bagels in Texas.'

'Great,' I said. 'So I'm joined at the hip to a guy who wears a coonskin cap without the tail and a dead man's shoes.'

'It could be worse,' said Ratso. 'There could be a dead man standing in your shoes.'

I got us both another round of espresso and extracted my first cigar of the morning from Sherlock Holmes's head.

'You know,' said Ratso, 'I wonder if these guys – these Colombians – could have been in this thing from the start. After all, you met Leila at the cat show. Then, very shortly after that, you're shot with a dart filled with a lethal dose of lion tranquilizer. And these guys, from everything I've read, aren't all that far removed from the jungle themselves.'

'I've considered that.' I lit the cigar and watched the smoke dance in the sunshine that was coming in the window. It was a cold but beautiful February day and there wasn't a Colombian in sight.

'And then,' Ratso continued, 'there's this Colombian necktie business.' My hand went unconsciously to my throat.

97

'Go on.'

'Well, I don't know if these guys have a tongue fetish or what, but there seems to be some common ground between the Colombian necktie and what happened to Rick 'Slick' Goldberg.'

'My dear Ratso, I don't know what I'd do without you.'

'So you think they iced Goldberg.'

'Actually, my conclusions are quite the opposite of that.'

'What do you mean?'

'I mean these are early days, Watson. Too early in the case to idly discuss it with you.'

'You're a sharing, caring kind of guy, Sherlock. It's inspiring to work with a guy who gives so much of himself.'

I puffed on the cigar a bit and looked at Ratso. 'As Marco Polo said on his deathbed in 1324: "I have not told one half of what I saw." '

'Yeah,' said Ratso, 'but those were the Dark Ages. Today inquiring minds want to know.'

'In this case,' I said, 'curiosity might just kill the rat.'

Not long thereafter, Ratso departed the loft in somewhat of a snit. I let him go. It was probably safer on the streets of New York than it was these days at 199B Vandam. Who the hell knows what's safe anymore? Some people claim the smoke from my cigar is drifting over to them and creating a health hazard, but I don't let it bother the Kinkster. The main health hazard in the world today is people who don't love themselves.

To cover all bases, I went to the desk, got the number of American Airlines, and gave it a call. All the American agents were busy so I had to listen to some tape-recorded Musak by the Captain and Toenail. Where were the Disappointer Sisters when you needed them?

It would be somewhat ironic if I were to net myself a

Colombian butterfly while waiting for the next available agent to answer the phone. For about two or three minutes I listened to the kind of crap that would make an elevator blush. Then I just said to hell with it.

40

The call that was going to change my life did not come that afternoon. There were two others, however.

The first was from Rambam, who felt I was laying my life on the line by not going to Texas. I told him I was laying my life on the line every time I ate a frankfurter at Madison Square Garden, but I wasn't leaving town because a cop and a private investigator were getting a little nervous in the service. He said something, probably to relieve his frustration and disgust, and then hung up.

It was a gorgeous day, as we say in New York, even if you're standing at the kitchen window of your loft anticipating that many men will come hurt you. The buildings looked gorgeous. The pigeons looked gorgeous. The prostitutes looked gorgeous. Actually, these things always have had an inherent beauty, but people have just tried too hard to look at them wrong. You come to see what you want to see.

I wanted to see this whole tension convention blow over. I wanted to continue with the case – find Slick Goldberg's killer, find Rocky. I wanted a lot of things and it didn't look like I was going to get them. I had about as much chance of coming out of this situation a happy American as Oliver Twist had of getting more.

The phone call that was to fling us headlong into something that nobody would think was gorgeous came at around three-fifteen that afternoon.

Interestingly enough, it was from Jane Meara.

99

41

It was Friday evening and the shadows were beginning to fall on Central Park as Ratso and I, who had reached at least some form of rapprochement, stood looking at a tall building on the corner of Seventh Avenue and Central Park South.

'Too bad,' said Ratso. 'We're only two blocks from the Carnegie Deli.'

'If we get through this alive, I'll buy you a bowl of matzo ball soup.'

'I really wanted a Reuben sandwich.'

'Fine.'

It was cold and dark and it was getting colder and darker and I was trying to explain to Ratso what we were doing there.

'Jane Meara called me today and she was quite distressed.'

'So what's new?'

'My dear Ratso, one would think you could dredge up a little more sensitivity for a person who's lost a cat.'

'Go on, Mr Sensitivity.'

'Well, Landis called Jane in and said her work was falling down since all this started, and Eugene was coarse enough to suggest she forget about Rocky and get a dog.'

'How thoughtless.' Ratso's eyes were straying in the direction of the Carnegie Deli.

'But the real reason we're here is that Jane was supposed to have lunch today with an editor from another publishing house whose name is Estelle Beekman. I know Estelle slightly myself. She's the author of a recent, critically acclaimed novel and she's sort of a recluse, but a very responsible person in the publishing business. She comes from an extremely wealthy family and she lives in this building. One of the things she wrote about in her novel is that she had been deathly afraid of cats since she was a child. To this day, she abhors them.'

'I like her already,' said Ratso. 'But why are we here?'

'She did not show up for her luncheon meeting with Jane, no one at her office knows where she is, and her telephone has been busy for about four hours now.'

'Maybe she's talking to her shrink about a Tom and Jerry cartoon she once saw when she was a child.'

'I don't think so, Ratso. There's no conversation on the line. I checked with the operator myself.'

'Why don't we call the police?'

'It may come to that, but with this broad and this building, Jane thought it might be better if we were to run a quick check on the situation first ourselves. We wouldn't want to create any social embarrassment, would we?'

'Of course not,' said Ratso in a voice that was possibly not quite as sincere as one would have hoped.

'Okay,' I said, 'there's about fifteen doormen and all of them are surly. I'm going to call a friend of mine who also lives here and then we'll go up and see the lay of the land.'

'The lay of the broad is what we'll probably see,' said Ratso.

'This is a very respectable broad, Ratso. She told me once that she hardly believes in social intercourse, much less sexual. I'll be right back.'

I went to a pay phone on the corner of Seventh Avenue next to the building and put in two bits. Nothing happened. No dial tone. No change. I took it in stride. The more storms one rides out in life, the better the captain one becomes of one's soul.

I tried the next pay phone. This wasn't easy because an escaped gorilla had ripped the receiver completely off the machine and left the wire dangling in the night air like the withered arm of a peasant.

The third pay phone worked fine and after three rings I got through to my friend. What hath God wrought?

Nick 'Chinga' Chavin, the guy I was calling in the building where Estelle Beekman lived, was a country singer turned ad exec. I knew the building, one of the poshest in New York, because I'd stayed a couple times with Chinga as his house pest there before I grew up and rented a loft and had to deal with house pests of my own.

One of the things Chinga liked to do late at night was to fire Chinese bottle rockets from his fourth-floor balcony at the New York Athletic Club just across Seventh Avenue. According to Chinga, the New York Athletic Club has, to this day, never admitted Jews or Negroes as members. They don't much like Chinese bottle rockets either. But on many occasions I'd witnessed Chinga laying siege to the club, aiming particularly at the Aryan shadows jogging along behind the tinted glass.

Now, Chinga agreed to call down to the concierge and tell him Ratso and I were his guests so we could get past the fifteen surly doormen.

He did and we did.

I told the elevator guy to take us to the sixteenth floor. We found the stairs, walked up three, didn't meet anyone. We wandered down a hallway awhile and found 19G, Estelle Beekman's apartment. The door was slightly ajar.

'Oh, shit,' I said, 'I don't like to see this.' I'd seen some things behind slightly ajar doors in my time, and none of them had turned out to be a free trip for two to Acapulco.

'What is it?' Ratso asked.

'We're about to find out,' I said.

I opened the door.

42

We walked in as gingerly as two astronauts stepping onto the moon. The place was quiet as a library and almost as big. We listened. There was a soft but persistent electronic sound coming from somewhere on our left. It was quiet and discreet, but it was there. Sort of like a coke dealer's beeper going off at a backgammon tournament.

We followed the sound for about half a mile and wound up in the kitchen. The telephone receiver was lying fornlornly on the drainboard. I took my snot rag out of my hip pocket, picked up the phone, and put it back on the hook. Sorry, nobody home.

We wandered back into the living room. It was dark, so we turned on a few lights. There were several big ornate lamps. There was track lighting. None of it removed the gloom, the visceral sense of foreboding that seemed to cover the pores like sweet, death-scented, coconut sun-tan oil. There was death all over the place. The only thing missing was the body.

Ratso and I made a cursory tour of the lushly furnished living room. It was like a rather macabre open house where you couldn't find the homeowner but you knew she must be hanging around somewhere. Or lying in one of the bedrooms. Or tied up.

There was expensive-looking chrome and leather furniture, Persian rugs, several large pieces of sculpture that must've meant something to somebody somewhere. Large vases, jade carvings.

'Jesus Christ,' said Ratso, gazing at a picture on the wall, 'look at that.'

'Yeah,' I said. 'That's nice.'

'You know what it is?'

'Sure,' I said. 'That's a picture of some fat naked ladies

dancing with each other.' I took a cigar out of one of the little stitched pockets on my hunting vest.

'It's a Matisse,' said Ratso.

'It's a triumph of art over life,' I said, as I lit the cigar.

'I'm glad you appreciate it,' said Ratso. I blew a cold stream of cigar smoke in the direction of the painting.

'I don't,' I said. 'I just think those fat, naked ladies dancing with each other have outlived Estelle Beekman.'

We walked from one posh room into another. No Estelle. Even the bathroom was something to see. She didn't have a twenty-seven-foot jade toilet seat like Kenny Rogers, but it was definitely a five-star pissoir.

'Since there's no dead body in the bathtub,' said Ratso, 'I think I'll use the facilities here.'

'Well, I'm sure it's all right with Estelle, wherever she is. It could be seen as a trifle gauche under the circumstances.'

'I've got to urinate like a racehorse.' Ratso unzipped his fly and I zipped out into the hallway.

'Don't whiz in the bidet,' I shouted through the partially closed door.

'I'm surprised you even know what that is.'

'Of course I do. Bidet lived a little before the time of Matisse. Many people feel that Matisse stole a lot of Bidet's ideas. Bidet had a splashy style and Matisse was kind of jealous – '

'All right,' shouted Ratso, 'that's enough. But what's she doing with a goddamned bidet if she doesn't believe in sexual intercourse?'

'We find her, we'll ask her,' I said. Never trust a person who's afraid of cats.

I walked into Estelle Beekman's bedroom and turned on the light. There was no dead body on the bed either, but lying on the floor there was a key that I didn't particularly

104

like the look of. I was about to pick it up when I heard a sound that turned my blood to Perrier on the rocks with a little twist of something I didn't need at all.

It was a cat's meow. It was coming from the closet.

I listened. It came again. It was joined by another meow.

Normally, the cat's meow does not turn my kneecaps to Smucker's. Even after the dart gun incident and the meow message on Jane Meara's answering machine, I had not felt that the voice of the cat could be, in itself, a manifestation of evil. Now, in this place, I wasn't so sure.

I got out my snot rag, picked up the key, and opened the locked door of the closet just as Ratso came walking in from the boudoir. For a moment, nothing happened. Then two scrawny street cats came toward us as if they were walking out of a Disney movie. One of them purred and rubbed itself against Ratso's legs. He moved away in disgust.

'What're these two cats doing in here?' Ratso fairly screamed.

'Maybe they're two homosexuals and they're just coming out of the closet,' I said.

I turned on the light switch in the closet with my snot rag. Nothing happened. I stepped inside the closet. Ratso followed. It was a big closet, crowded with furs and long evening gowns, and it wasn't easy to see with the subdued lighting of the bedroom. I took out my Bic and I gave it a flick.

What we saw on the floor of the closet did not look like a Disney movie at all. It looked more like something brought to you by the people who killed Bambi's mother.

Estelle Beekman's eyes were wide as shiny new nickels, and they reflected pure, polyunsaturated terror. The body was already cold to the touch. The face was blue; the throat muscles looked constricted. One hand had scratched the wall repeatedly in several places, somewhat reminiscent of wall markings I'd heard about elsewhere. For a moment I had a fragment of a picture of an old man walking into a gas chamber playing a violin. Then the Bic became too hot and I let it go.

A few minutes later, I'd opened the sliding door to the private balcony and we were breathing the cold night air and looking down on the New York Athletic Club.

'Let a little of the cigar-smoke out of here,' I said. 'When I call the police I'm going to strive for anonymity.'

'So she was frightened to death,' said Ratso. 'Killed by two cats.'

'More likely by Fred Katz. Or the person we think is Fred Katz.'

For a few minutes we watched a horse and buggy and a driver in a top hat fighting their way through the taxis, buses, and limos down Seventh Avenue. Happy trails.

Ratso was shaking his head, leaning on the railing. 'Literally frightened to death,' he mumbled, half to himself, half to Central Park.

I didn't say anything.

'It's a shame,' Ratso said. 'Estelle Beekman leaving behind all that beautiful shit she's got in there.'

We'd only been out on the balcony for a few minutes, but I was feeling colder than I had in years.

I took a last puff on the cigar and flicked it across Seventh Avenue at the New York Athletic Club.

'You never see a luggage rack on a hearse,' I said.

43

It was after eleven when Ratso and I climbed out of the hack a few blocks past Sheridan Square and began walking briskly up Vandam Street. It had been a rather gnarly night, cold enough to make a penguin remember his mittens, and it wasn't over yet.

I'd asked Ratso to put a sock on it conversation-wise, so I could use the walk home to sort things out a bit. Sometimes a walk in brutal weather could freeze extraneous sensory input and make you AWOL upstairs, leaving you with the ice-cold truth. Sometimes all you got was a runny nose. But that, along with not leaving fingerprints, was what snot rags were for.

I let my mind run free. I thought of Eskimos. Two Eskimos rubbing their noses together. Nine months later they'd probably have a little booger. I thought of icebergs. I thought of Goldberg. Goldberg had liked cats. He'd been killed. Estelle Beekman had been afraid of cats. She'd been killed. Jane Meara loved cats. Her life, it appeared, was in danger.

Something was wrong here, I thought. I'd have to call Lobster and find out more about Slick Goldberg. Maybe cats weren't the common denominator here. If not – what was? . . . And Leila . . . why in the hell hadn't she called? I knew she might be lying low after the bust and the *Daily News* story, but I missed her. Maybe even . . .

'Kinkster,' said Ratso suddenly, 'the fucking door to the building's open.'

It was true. It was nudging eleven-thirty at night and the large metal door to the building was standing wide open. You left a door open in New York, you'd be lucky if a family of Rastafarians was all you got.

'Could be a careless lesbian,' I said.

As we rode up in the freight elevator with the one exposed light bulb, the hairs on the back of my neck began to rise as well. I was visited by a trapped, desperate, doomed feeling. It's hard to run away when you're in a freight elevator.

'Next time,' I said, 'remind me to take the stairs.'

'If there is a next time,' said Ratso.

When the doors opened on the fourth floor we fairly leaped out of the elevator into the dimly lit hallway. I already had my key in the door of the loft when something made me stop. I looked back and saw Ratso standing stiff in his coonskin cap in the middle of the hallway like a chunky, slightly Semitic statue of Davy Crockett. With his right hand, he was pointing at the door.

On the door to the loft was a paw print of what looked like a jaguar or a large jungle cat. It was red and still dripping and, almost certainly, done in blood.

'Careless lesbian?' Ratso asked.

'Maybe somebody knocked too hard,' I said.

44

In pre-Colombian times, life was much simpler.

That was the thought that was in my head when I woke up early Saturday morning with a ringing in my ears. It was the blower.

I grabbed the blower and looked at the clock by the bedside. It was 6.15 a.m., a fairly obscene time for anybody to be awake. It was also, it emerged, a fairly obscene phone call.

'I want you,' said Leila. She sounded like she was right next to me in bed with no guitar case between us.

'Do I have your little heart in my hip pocket?' I asked. That was as coy as I got at six-fifteen in the morning.

'Yes,' she said, 'but I have you right here.'

'Where's here?'

'I'll give you a hint – it's right where I want you.'

Great waves of passion rolled over me. I didn't know if it was Leila's Palestinian, Colombian, or New York background that enabled her to have such an effect on me. All three cultures seem to have sort of a jaded, hedonistic attitude towards love and sex. Thank God I'm a country boy.

'Hold the weddin',' I said.

'Wedding?' said Leila. 'This is awful sudden. I need some time. If we do get married, though, I think I'm going to make you wear a veil.' She laughed confidently.

'Castrating bitch.'

'I'm not a castrating bitch,' she said. 'I just want the West Bank.'

'It's yours,' I said, 'if you promise to always walk ten steps behind me.' I got out of bed, took off the sarong, and put on some jeans. I managed to zip them up without killing myself.

'Honey,' said Leila, 'Carlos promised me he's not going to hurt you. He may just try to scare you a little.'

'Yeah,' I said. 'He scared me a little last night.'

'Don't worry, my brother won't hurt you. They're having some kind of meeting tonight, but I'll keep you posted. Everything's going to be all right.'

'Where are you?' I asked.

There was a pause. Finally, Leila said, 'I'm with my Uncle Abdul – don't laugh, that's not his real name. I have to be very careful just now. We can't be seen together. There is another family that hates our family and would do anything to harm me and those I love.'

'Okay, Juliet.'

'It is a little like that, isn't it?'

'Yeah,' I said, 'except all the warring families are on your side.'

'I don't want to get you in any trouble. I don't want anything to happen to you. And Kinky – '

'What?'

'I think I love you.'

There was a long pause and Leila might've been crying.

As I hung up, I wondered why I couldn't just meet a broad at the mailbox on the day her Visa card arrived. Why did things always have to be so melodramatic and convoluted?

'One of these days,' I said to the cat, 'they're going to make a life out of my movie.'

45

Maybe I should've driven my car into a tree in high school, but I didn't. Jesus or Allah or somebody wanted me to be drinking hot chocolate in a drafty loft and watching freezing rain slant down by the window at 8 a.m. that Saturday morning. I thought I'd give the espresso machine a rest. When you drink too much espresso, you think too much. When you think too much, you can't see the forest for the tree you should've driven your car into in high school.

I felt I was close to achieving peace in the Middle East, but no matter what I felt for Leila, I couldn't let her assessment of her brother, Carlos, determine whether I was to live or die. According to her, Carlos was merely a macho practical joker. He had nothing better to do than go around scaring people who weren't too secure to begin with.

What if she didn't know her brother as well as she thought she did? Maybe because she loved him, she couldn't see what he really was. Maybe because she thought she loved me, she was shielding me from the truth. Maybe because I thought I loved her I was placing myself, Ratso, the cat, and an innocent lesbian dance class in grave danger.

That didn't say much for love.

Something else was bothering me, too. I tongued a few more mini-marshmallows out of the hot chocolate. Had to keep in practice. I ate the marshmallows and thought about it. The bloody paw print on the door. I'd seen it before somewhere.

I fed the cat some tuna. They say if you feed a cat tuna all the time, you'll turn the cat into a tuna addict. Makes the cat finicky and irritable. I say, 'How can you tell?' My cat happens to have always been finicky and irritable and I've always been finicky and irritable and we don't need other people telling us how to run our lives.

Hot chocolate and mini-marshmallows go well with cigars and rain. Of course, just about anything goes well with cigars and rain except asparagus tips or whatever they call them. Bean sprouts. I was sitting in the rocker, working on hot chocolate number three and cigar number one and watching Ratso sleep, when I remembered where I'd seen the red paw print.

So as not to wake Ratso, I padded quietly, like a jungle cat, over to the desk. Then I picked up the blower on the left and dialed a number in Austin, Texas.

46

Back when Margaret Mead was jumping rope in the school-yard, Jim Bone and I had taken Anthropology 301 together at the University of Texas at Austin. Of course, now he was Dr Jim Bone, but I didn't hold that against him. Jim had retained everything he'd learned in the anthropological field, traveled the world, and gone on to become one of the foremost experts on ancient, obscure, and lost cultures. I'd repressed everything I learned, traveled the world, and become a country singer who, some cynics would say, is probably also an expert on lost culture.

Jim had spent considerable time exploring in South America and had been the first white man to do a lot of things. One of them was hosing a piñata. It was only

7.30 a.m., Texas time, but in New York, I had the spiritually debilitating feeling that time was running out.

'Jimbo! Leap sideways!' I said. 'Somebody put a red paw print on the door of my loft.'

Jim sounded a big grumpy but coherent. 'Bit obsolete,' he said. 'People haven't been doing that for a thousand years.'

'Yeah, well, somebody did it to me last night.'

'I'll tell you what it's *not*,' he said.

'What?'

'A "Happy Bar Mitzvah" sign.'

What followed was a long and somewhat ill bout of laughter. Only idiots or geniuses laughed that way at seven-thirty in the morning. It was dealer's choice.

When the maniacal laughter had subsided, Jim gave me a crash course on the lowland Wachíchi many of whom had been jaguar priests, and all of whom appeared to have vanished from the face of the earth in the space of one week, over a thousand years ago.

The Wachíchi worshiped a god called Kukulcán, the cat god, who some believe was an early spaceman, and who disappeared into the skies forever in 986 AD. The Wachíchi were seagoing colonists, contemporaries of the Aztecs, Incas, Babylonians, and ancient Romans. The tradition of wearing masks so the sun couldn't see their faces originated with the Wachíchi, was later borrowed by the Iroquois, and was even later taken on by many disingenuous Americans who still didn't wish the sun to see their faces.

The jaguar priests of the Wachíchi, in their darker moments, were said to dress up as cats. It is known that they dealt with the structure of evil, not the structure of accomplishment. The information, according to Dr Bone, comes from the *Chilam Balam*, which are roughly the New World equivalent of the Dead Sea Scrolls – except, again according to Dr Bone, that they are about one hundred times spookier.

'So you've become involved with a cat lately,' Jim said.

'You've been readin' my mail, brother. Several weeks ago a friend of mine's cat disappeared during a cat show at Madison Square Garden and very little's been the same since.'

'Sounds about right. Any South or Central American types in your life currently?'

'You're battin' a thousand.'

'Are they maybe Colombians or Peruvians – ?'

'Colombians.'

'Sorry to hear that.'

'So am I.'

'Let me get a cup of coffee. Hold the line. I want to think about this for a moment.'

While Dr Jim Bone got a cup of coffee in Austin, Texas, I took the opportunity to move smoothly into hot chocolate number four and to perform the prenuptial arrangements on cigar number two. I lit the cigar and tongued a few more mini-marshmallows. There was a certain sweet afterglow to the combination that I'd never felt before in my life. Jim was back on the line.

'No one knows for sure,' he said, 'what happened to the Wachíchi. Did they disappear? Did they sail somewhere and recolonize? But around 1000 A.D. the Norse fought many wars with a group they called the cat people. This occurred in the New York-New England area. One of the results was a tribe of Indians that spoke a combination of Old Norse and Quiché. Quiché, of course, was the language of the Wachíchi.'

'This is,' I said, 'no doubt fascinating. But how is it relevant?' This is one of the problems you encounter in dealing

113

with anthropologists and archaeologists. They prefer the past to the present. How stupid of them.

'What I'm trying to establish in your adult brain,' Jim said rather irritably, 'is that there is a long tradition for the Wachíchi to be visiting New York City.'

'Unpleasant,' I said.

'Not from an anthropological view.'

'Fine.'

'I'm not trying to scare you, but people have traveled a lot farther for a lot stupider reasons than finding a cat.'

'Certainly this is a bit farfetched.'

'Jason and the Golden Fleece. The quest for the Holy Grail. Hell, the Egyptians went all the way to Tunisia for a missing finger ring. It's not that strange.'

It was that strange.

Art Linkletter was right, I thought. People *are* funny. Of course, they're not quite as funny as Art Linkletter, but they're funny enough to make you die laughing.

'Listen to me,' he said. 'Can't you understand this? Am I here alone? Am I driving through a ghost town? You may be on the verge of a major anthropological discovery.'

One of the little difficulties with the world is that it's riddled with anthropologists who travel to the far corners of the earth and bore people with their theories. My father once told me that in Greenland every family has five kids, three dogs, two chickens, and one anthropologist.

'Like what?' I asked. 'Finding a fossilized turd in the litter box?'

Dr Jim Bone was not amused. 'Wake up, man. Don't you know what that red cat strike on the door means?'

'That's why I called you, Jim.'

'Well, I'll tell you,' he said evenly. 'That's the standard Wachíchi mark of death.'

'I'll jot that down in my field notes,' I said. But I knew I wouldn't have to jot it down to remember it. If I'd had any field notes and if I'd tried jotting something down in them, I couldn't've been sure my hand wouldn't shake.

'That cat you're looking for,' said Jim. 'The one that's missing. That cat wouldn't have four white paws, would it?'

I felt like an ancient civilization had come crumbling down on top of me while I'd been out in the field looking for arrowheads. For a moment I was speechless, a rare occurrence indeed. Then that good old twentieth-century indifference came roaring back. Man is nothing if not resilient. Only sometimes there's little enough to be resilient about.

Four little white sweat socks, I thought.

'How,' I asked, 'in the name of Kukulcán, did you know that?'

'Because the Wachíchi had another name for Kukulcán.'

'Yeah? What?'

'They sometimes called him,' said Dr Jim Bone, 'the God Who Stands with His Feet in the Clouds.'

47

The telephone works in mysterious ways. Sometimes it brings you cheerful little insipid greetings from cheerful little insipid people. Sometimes it leaves you just a little to the north of scared shitless.

I was cleaning the red paw print of Kukulcán off the door of the loft with hot water and Ajax when Ratso almost stumbled on the bucket on his way into the bathroom.

'What the fuck are you doin'?' he asked. 'You're gonna want lab tests, aren't you?'

'The only thing I want a lab test on is your brain,' I said a bit unkindly.

'Yeah, but if it's human blood, or animal blood, that might tell us something.'

'It's already told us something,' I said. I gave Ratso a quick rundown on the phone call I'd had with Jim Bone. When I finished he tried to whistle but it was too early in the morning. He settled for looking pale.

'The last thing the cops want to hear,' I said as I continued washing off the blood, 'is some yarn about ancient civilizations. Cops are not anthropologists. They find other ways of being tedious.'

'I still don't think you should've washed it off.'

'It's either that or look at the son of a bitch every time I come in. It's probably nothing anyway.'

Ratso didn't look convinced.

As I paced up and down the loft and listened to him gargle, cough, and flush the toilet about seven times, I didn't think I was too convinced either. All of us will be relics someday, I thought. Let's just hope somebody nice finds us. It was probably too much to ask that somebody nice should find us while we're still alive.

Ratso came out of the bathroom, got dressed, and put on a pair of telephone repairman's rubber boots that almost went up to his waist.

'I hate rain,' he said.

'I love the rain,' I said.

The cat, who was sleeping peacefully on the rocker, didn't say anything, but it was safe to say, I thought, that she loved the rain, too.

I looked at the open door of the loft. There was still a ghostly shadow where the red paw print had been. It didn't look like the kind of thing Ajax and hot water would get rid of. I doubted if Mr Clean was going to cut much ice either. I was going to have to get a new door or a new loft.

No matter what I did, I had the feeling the ghostly shadow

would always be there. If not on the door, in the nightmare of my mind's eye.

48

The snow was beginning to mix with the rain as Ratso and I walked along Twelfth Street that Saturday night. It was just a little after eight o'clock and young men were picking up young women for dining engagements. Young men were picking up young men for dining engagements. Young women were picking up young women for dining engagements. You are what you eat.

It was Saturday night. It was the Village. It was America. It was 1988. It was cold. About the only thing it wasn't, was very pleasant. In the far reaches of my peripheral vision I could see a specter lurking. I could feel the frostbitten wings of angels occasionally brushing against my cowboy hat. Something besides rain, snow, cheap perfume, and roasting chestnuts was in the air. It was death – possibly the only dinner guest more unwelcome than Sidney Poitier.

As we crossed Fifth Avenue, the rain seemed to let up and the snow began to fall more heavily. In the white-and-gray dimness I could just make out the giant iguana on the roof of the Lone Star Cafe one block up the street. It stood like a beacon to rather ill pilgrims. Even in that weather, I felt the chill it gave me.

It'd been a little over a year ago that I'd played the Lone Star. It had been the performance of my life and damn nearly the last performance of my life. Now everything was back to normal at the Lone Star except that Cleve was sending me postcards from the mental hospital, and when I wanted a waiter to bring my check I seldom used the phrase 'Drop the hatchet' anymore.

On the other side of Fifth, a cat jumped out of a garbage

can. From force of habit, I tailed him a little way down the block. It wasn't Rocky. Kind of hard to keep your mind on a missing cat when you knew that soon you might be missing your lungs.

We banked a sharp left in the middle of Twelfth between Fifth and University and went down a few steps and through a couple doors into Asti's Italian restaurant, where the waiters, bartenders, busboys, and the guy that checks your hat and coat all sing opera.

As we came in the place, Augie, the owner, was behind the bar banging out 'Dixie' on the rows of bottles. Then he moved over to the cash register and played a few more choruses, using the keys to ring up the melody and sliding the cash drawer in and out for percussion.

'Versatile,' said Ratso to a group of well-dressed European tourists. They looked at him like they thought he'd just flown in from the coast and hadn't bothered to take a plane.

Saturday night is not the best night to go to Asti's. There're a few too many tourists from Iowa, Japan, and the Upper West Side. But if it wasn't for tourists in New York, they'd probably have to close the Empire State Building, the Staten Island ferry, and the Statue of Liberty, because the locals would stay away in droves.

My knowledge of opera extends to *The Student Prince*, which I know isn't really opera but is very good, and sometimes *La Bohelme*. Asti's draws heavily from both of these, some show tunes, some long-haired, fat-lady type songs that are good to get drunk by, and medleys of things like 'Dixie,' 'When Irish Eyes Are Smiling,' and 'Hava Nagila,' which say something to everyone but Japanese businessmen.

Asti's was founded by Augie's father on the date Caruso died. You can't urinate in the place without coming face to face with autographed photos of Toscanini sailing for

118

America and Caruso singing an aria. Augie assures me Caruso did not die after he ate there.

Augie finished playing the cash register to thunderous applause and showed the Rat and me to a table near the small stage. Vittorio, in his little Russian cap, was singing 'If I Were a Rich Man' when a large form came lumbering up to our table.

'May I join you girls?' it asked. It was McGovern.

'How the hell did you know we were here?' I said a bit irritably.

'Got a tip from Reuters,' said McGovern, as he sat down with us and ordered a Vodka McGovern from a passing waiter. 'That's vodka, orange juice, soda, with lime. Vodka McGovern.'

'No problem,' said the waiter.

'I'll have a Vodka McGovern, too,' said Ratso.

'I'll have some kind of obscure, expensive cognac,' I said. It was a good thing to warm the blood and I wasn't happy enough with McGovern to order a Vodka McGovern, or even to eat one of my favorite dishes he cooked, Chicken McGovern. In the back of my mind still lurked, despite his denials, the thought that my old pal might've put my life in jeopardy.

'So tell me,' said McGovern, 'about that giant red claw mark you found on the door of your loft. That must've scared the shit out of you two.'

I looked at Ratso and Ratso looked at me. We both shrugged.

'How'd you know about that?' Ratso asked, suddenly nervous.

'I have sources,' McGovern laughed, 'among the gay terpischorean community.'

'Goddamn poufters,' said Ratso.

'Alarmingly homophobic,' I said, as I sipped a little of

119

the obscure and expensive cognac.' As Rita Mae Brown says, "If Michelangelo had been a heterosexual, the Sistine Chapel would have been painted basic white with a roller." '

Ratso looked at me. 'I didn't know you were into such highbrow writers,' he said.

I sipped the cognac. It tasted like semiviscous airplane fuel from the Amelia Earhart era. I didn't respond.

'Better than no brow at all,' said McGovern.

49

I was working on a linguine with red clam sauce when Pasquale hit the stage simultaneously singing Figaro and demonstrating how to make a pizza. He threw the spinning dough in the air repeatedly until it reached a diameter of about three feet. Then he put it on his head like a scarf and sang a verse of 'Don't Cry for Me, Argentina.'

Pasquale now tore little balls of dough from the pizza and threw them to various diners seated around the place. Eddie, the piano player, kicked into high gear and the patrons threw the dough balls back toward Pasquale, who, holding a tambourine in front of his face like a hoop, caught them in his teeth.

Through this hall of dough balls walked a figure in a business suit carrying an attacheк case. It sat down at our table and ordered a double shot of Bushmills. It was Rambam.

He set the attacheк case down on the floor beside his chair and reached across the table to take one of Ratso's Shrimp Puccini.

'I like your Wall Street drag,' said Ratso.

'Not everybody has your vast wardrobe, Ratso,' I said.

'And not everybody wants to go around looking like a Sonny Bono impersonator,' said Rambam.

'Is that why you're affecting that attaché case?' Ratso said.

'No,' Rambam laughed, 'that's my Uzi sub-machine gun.' He took the double Bushmills with one large gulp. 'Not bad,' he said.

At the next table were some opera buffs. One guy was pretty friendly and gave me periodic little nods when a song was performed particularly well. I could kind of cue off of him so I knew how much enthusiasm to applaud and bravo with. He probably took me for an eccentric but willing-to-learn non-opera buff in my cowboy hat, for we exchanged knowing little nods throughout the course of the evening.

There existed, of course, the possibility that he was a homosexual. But opera buffs, like cowboys, are probably a dying breed in this busy world and whatever they choose to do is okay with me. If you ever had to sleep with one of them in the same bed, it might be smart, however, to put a cello case between you.

Augie came by the table. 'Would you gentlemen like a round of drinks on the house?' he asked.

It was an offer McGovern couldn't refuse and he appeared as happy as a young gentile on Christmas morning. None of us refused the offer, actually, but some of us were more subdued in our enthusiasm. In a world of empty gestures, coming from Augie at Asti's, this was a real one.

'Shall I check that briefcase for you?' he asked Rambam.

'No, he'll keep it,' Ratso said delightedly. 'It's his Uzi submachine gun.'

Augie laughed. Rambam laughed. McGovern laughed. Even the opera buff at the next table laughed. I went to the men's room to grab a Republican by the neck and watch Arturo Toscanini sail to America.

When I returned to the table, Rambam was on the subject of South American hit men. 'Dixie cup kids,' he said. 'That's what they call them. Completely expendable. Anything happens to 'em, they buy their family a few acres and a couple of pigs and everybody's happy.'

'This conversation's off the record, of course,' I said to McGovern.

'Of course,' said McGovern, his eyes twinkling.

Before we left, we said goodbye to the opera buffs, the piano player, Vittorio, Pasquale, several bartenders and waiters, and, of course, Augie. It was like leaving home. And, unlike Gallagher's Steak House, Asti's lets you wear your hat indoors if you're a cowboy. One of the few things cowboys and Jews have in common is that they both wear their hats indoors and attach a certain amount of importance to it. Hank Williams wore his hat indoors. So did Davy Crockett. A friend of mine, Bob McLane, who was the former chairman of the Gay Texans for Bush Committee, told me that George Bush always took his hat off when he came inside a place. That's another good reason for wearing a hat indoors.

Ratso and McGovern, having already hosed me on the check, were up front getting their coats. I was still dealing with the check, paying the guy at the other cash register, the one that didn't play 'Dixie' but just took your money. Ratso circled back briefly, requested and received a receipt for the meal I was paying for, and walked back to the door. Sometimes Ratso could take the word *chutzpah* to a whole other level.

Rambam was having a last drink at the bar as I walked by to get my coat.

'Have one with me for the road,' he said.

As I ordered a shot of Jameson, I noticed his attaché case resting on the barstool next to him. 'What *is* in the attaché case?' I asked.

In the background a man and a woman were dancing

together on the stage and singing a duet of 'The Surrey with the Fringe on Top.' Rambam watched the stage with a far-away expression. When he spoke he had all the even-mindedness of the Mahatma.

'An Uzi submachine gun,' said Rambam.

50

We were standing outside Asti's on the sidewalk. McGovern, Ratso, myself, Rambam, and Rambam's attacheκ case. Either the music and the magic of Asti's was staying with me or it was the red clam sauce.

We drifted with the snow down toward Fifth Avenue. My thoughts skittered like snowflakes through all the cold nights and all the winters of the past. I was wearing my old blue David Copperfield greatcoat that I'd had forever and that Ratso'd always coveted. I'd bought it down the street from the Greyhound station in Albany, New York, shortly after I'd been deselected from my first Peace Corps program. I thought of Leila with her David Copperfield cap. Maybe someday, if we both lived long enough, we'd take off our David Copperfield clothes and put them together in a warm closet somewhere. Then we could twist away the summer. Be happy Americans. Raise cute, gypsylike children who'd grow up realizing that their parents loved each other. I put my hands down into the big pockets of the coat.

There was something in the right pocket that hadn't been there when I'd left 199B Vandam. It was a package of some sort, but I didn't like surprises and I didn't think it was my birthday.

I took the parcel out and looked at it. It was the size of a thin brick or maybe a somewhat undernourished video-cassette. It was wrapped in brown butcher paper and tied with twine. Scrawled in pencil on the butcher paper were the words PERLA YI-YO.

'Maybe it's a valentine present that's a little slow out of the chute,' said Ratso. He grabbed the package out of my hand.

'Gimme that,' said Rambam. He took the package from Ratso and headed back in the direction of Asti's with it. About halfway there, he found a doorway with steps leading down below ground level. Rambam took out a knife and disappeared from sight.

Ratso, McGovern, and I stood around the little doorway watching Rambam down on the ground fooling with the package. 'Under the circumstances,' he said, 'this could be a bomb.'

'Why don't you see if it's ticking?' Ratso said.

'That big-alarm-clock shit went out with the Russian Revolution, Ratso,' said Rambam. 'Today, they use a little Timex or something – you couldn't even hear it until it's too late.'

'If it's our guys,' I said, 'they probably used a Rolex.'

'Very funny,' said Rambam, as he gingerly poked the knife into the side of the package. 'You want to be very careful, you see, not to mess with the twine. We'll know in a minute . . . one way or another.'

I looked over at Ratso and he wasn't there. One moment he was standing between McGovern and myself, and the next moment there was nothing but McGovern's large head blocking out Fifth Avenue.

'Maybe you should call the bomb squad,' came a voice from about forty feet away. Ratso was standing in the street on the other side of a parked car.

'Hate cops,' said Rambam.

'Maybe you should put those feelings aside,' said McGovern, 'till this whole thing blows over.'

'An unfortunate use of words,' I said. 'I'm concerned about your use of the language, McGovern. You know what Hemingway said about journalism, don't you?'

'What'd he say?' asked McGovern as both of us backed slightly away from the doorway.

'He said, "It blunts your instrument." '

'And hanging around a bullring can sap your semen,' said McGovern.

'Holy shit,' said Rambam. McGovern and I moved a little farther away. Rambam might be right or he might be off the wall, but it'd be pretty ugly if all of us were to wind up literally off the wall.

'What is it?' called Ratso.

'Come over here and find out,' I said.

McGovern and I inched a little closer to the doorway. Rambam had cut a small hole in the side of the package. He'd cut through the butcher paper and through a thick layer of plastic, revealing what looked like a white chemical substance.

'What the hell is it?' asked McGovern.

'Could be potassium chlorate,' said Rambam, 'a very popular ingredient in explosives today.'

It was about at this time that I put my hand back into my coat pocket and found the little card that had apparently fallen off the package.

'Hold the weddin',' I said. 'It ain't a bomb. Take a look at this. It's a note that came with the package.'

Rambam, knife in hand, came over to me. So did McGovern. Even Ratso found his way back from the street and looked over my shoulder at the little card. It read as follows:

I hope you enjoy this little token of my gratitude. I have

125

great admiration for what you have done. Soon I shall meet you.

The Jaguar

'Nice-looking business card,' I said.

51

I was standing on a sidewalk in the Village at 11.30 p.m. on a Saturday night, holding in my hands a brick of cocaine whose street value, when cut, would probably exceed a quarter of a million dollars. Want a toot?

I'd been in the presence of that much cocaine before on several occasions, though I doubted if the quality had been commensurate with the current batch. Once in LA, I'd been sort of house-sitting for a rather shady friend who was off somewhere in the Caribbean. I knew the guy had a few too many Tiffany lamps but I didn't figure it out until I stumbled on a large briefcase full of off-white rocks the size of puppet heads.

Years later, I'd related this story to a well-traveled, coke-dealing Brit in my hotel room in New York and he had not been too impressed. 'I've seen the factory, mate,' he said.

'Let Ratso hold that shit,' said Rambam. The two of them whispered back and forth as my hands trembled.

'Obviously, the Jaguar is Carlos's bitter enemy and believes what he reads in the *Daily News*,' I said, looking pointedly at McGovern.

'I'm not Deep Throat,' said McGovern.

Fortunately, the weather was keeping side-walk traffic to a minimum, but it was still a very strange feeling holding what could surely be my certain death and destruction in my hands. Of course, I'd have some fun before I'd go.

'Better let one of us keep it,' said Rambam, like he was talking to a child.

'C'mon,' I said. 'I haven't touched the stuff in almost seventy-two hours now. I had to quit when Bob Marley fell out of my left nostril.' I was breaking out in a sweat.

I had torn off some more of the butcher paper and the plastic and run a little taste test to establish that it wasn't potassium chlorate. It wasn't.

I gripped the packet tightly until Ratso took it away from me. But I remember gazing at it under the streetlamp. It looked as beautiful as fish scales in the moonlight.

And memories came back to me like snow falling on snow.

52

Sunday started as a busy day on the blower and ended with my almost getting blown away. But first things first.

I got up, fought back a desire to strangle Ratso to find where he'd hid the cocaine, thought better of it, and made some espresso. No point in having hot chocolate. It wasn't raining.

I fed the cat. Tuna in any weather.

I walked over to the desk with the espresso and sat down. When I took the top off Sherlock Holmes's head to get a cigar, I looked inside to see if Ratso had stashed the cocaine in there. Of course, it was a ridiculous notion, but there you are. It wasn't there. Neither were Sherlock's brains and I had the feeling I was going to be needing them before this mess was over. I would deal with the Jaguar when he came. I would deal with Carlos when he came. I would deal with Leila when she came. A man's not a man until he's given multiple orgasms to a Palestinian terrorist. Of course, Leila wasn't a real terrorist, but she had done some things under a comforter that damn near scared me. I'd been the comforter, of course.

The first call I made was to a colorful, mysterious friend of mine named Dangerous Dan, who was an authority on powders, the Latin American import-export business, and just about everything else that nobody really knows about. Since I spoke to Dangerous, he has left us and gone to Jesus, and I hope and trust that he's made heaven a happier place since he's arrived. But if somehow he got de-selected from heaven, I've always felt I could do a lot worse than waking up in hell next to Dangerous Dan.

Dangerous said that *perla* meant 'pearl' and *yi-yo* was an Indian word that did not compute into the white man's mind. Taken together, he said, they meant 'the best of the best.' Where had I seen that phrase? he wanted to know. I told him the men's room at the Lone Star Cafe. Which stall? he wanted to know. There was only one stall, I told him. He told me to be careful. I told him I'd do my best.

I miss Dangerous Dan and I think of him, in human terms, as perla yi-yo.

I didn't know what Dangerous Dan thought of cats, but Slick Goldberg had liked cats and Estelle Beekman had hated cats and someone had killed them both. So what did that tell us? Not a damn thing. Or maybe it did.

For the next half hour I made a series of calls to information operators in Connecticut, finally hit pay dirt, and called my party. Things were just about what I'd expected. We talked for a while and arranged to get together in the city soon for a drink.

Forty-five minutes is a long time to be on the blower but I was used to hard work. Anyway, the alternative was to look around the loft for some perla yi-yo that I didn't really want to find, because it would fry my remaining synapses in about four seconds and then they would be holding memorial services for my brain in New York and Los Angeles. I got another cigar and another espresso and I made my last call of the day to Jane Meara.

I told her she wouldn't be having lunch with Estelle Beekman anymore. I gave it to her pretty straight. She held up as well as could be expected. In fact, she was starting to show a toughness I didn't know she had.

I told her if the cops called her, and I didn't think they would, she never talked to me about Estelle Beekman. She said she understood.

I asked her if there'd been any news on Rocky from her end. She ticked off an extensive list of everything she'd done to find her. Net result: no Rocky.

I was reading Jane a story from the *National Enquirer* about a cat named Tom who'd walked 773 miles from Harrison, Arkansas, to his home in Detroit, when I noticed that Sleeping Beauty had awakened from the couch and was walking toward the television set with a screwdriver in his hand. I told Jane to be very careful. I had a few little problems of my own right now, but we'd wrap this whole business up quite soon, I was sure. There wasn't much else to say, and it wouldn't have been very easy anyway because Ratso had, by this time, turned the set up quite loud.

I walked over to where Ratso was sitting and looked at the screen. Many men carrying long sticks were moving rapidly across a great expanse of frozen tundra. At either end, there was a large figure wearing a Wachíchi mask.

'Ranger game!' Ratso shouted.

53

By Sunday afternoon at four-thirty, Ratso, myself, Rambam, and Rambam's attaché case were having lunch at Big Wong on Mott Street in Chinatown. Just before I'd left the loft,

Leila had called. She had not heard from her brother Carlos as she had expected, and she was worried. She knew the feds had not picked him up in the bust and she couldn't understand why he hadn't contacted her. I told her if I saw him I'd tell him to call her.

There followed a conversation of a rather sweet and personal nature that was rudely punctuated by Ratso's loud and prolonged curses as the Rangers lost the hockey game. Apparently Ratso'd taped the game at his apartment the previous evening and brought his VCR over to the loft. Nice to see him staying on top of things.

Big Wong was like dying and going to heaven at this time of the day. It wasn't crowded, the food was great, and the waiters treated us like old friends, doing humorous things like bringing Ratso one chopstick. Ratso never found this to be very funny, but I always got a good chuckle out of it. Rambam thought it was pretty funny, too. I don't know what Rambam's attaché case thought. It was sitting in its own chair, not saying anything. I didn't know it at the time, but it would be talking a blue streak before the night was over.

Big Wong is a little different from most places in Chinatown. It isn't fancy and the menu is not very extensive and not very expensive. The food could be equated to that at a very good all-night truck stop, if the Chinese culture had such things as truck stops, country music jukeboxes, and rubber machines, which of course it does not. It does have Big Wong.

But occasional honky faces are beginning to pop up among the clientele these days. Soon some guy with a bow tie from *The New York Times* will stumble onto the place, write a trendy little piece on it, give it a couple of stars, and it'll all be over. When that happens, you might as well order out from Eggroll King in Columbus, Ohio.

It was starting to get dark by the time we got out of Big Wong. We walked down the sidewalks of Chinatown past ducks hanging upside down in the shop windows, past the Chinese dwarf painting pastel pictures of a distant home-land, past the fish markets along the sidewalk, past stalls selling strange-looking vegetables that appeared as if they'd been grown on another planet.

At this time of day and at this time of year the city was gray. But there was something very vital about things that were East. You could see, hear, and smell them, and they renewed the senses and the spirit. The whole scene was reminiscent of the time I'd spent in Kuching, the capital of Sarawak in Borneo. *Kuching* was a Malay word, I reflected as we crossed Canal Street, that, interestingly enough, meant 'cat.'

We walked up Mulberry Street, bought a few cigars at Louie's. Louie said, 'Hey, it's Buffalo Bill. Look, there he is,' he said to the other customers in the little shop, mostly elderly Chinese buying lottery tickets, 'the Gene Autry of Canal Street.' I wasn't sure if Rambam appreciated Louie as much as Ratso and I did. Rambam was half Italian and Louie was about as close to home as you could get without somebody telling you to take out the trash.

We had cappuccino, espresso, and cannoli at a little side-walk café next to a store that sold Mussolini T-shirts.

'One thing I have very little use for,' I said, 'is a Mussolini T-shirt.'

'Neither does Mussolini,' said Ratso, as he took a rather large bite of cannoli.

In the growing dark we walked through SoHo past stores that sold nothing but pillows, and a ghost town of galleries and industrial lofts taken over by narrow-tied, suspendered New Wave artists. A small group of musicians played chamber music inside a restaurant that served Art Deco chicken-fried steak. SoHo was one of the last places on earth where a break dancer could still draw a crowd.

The closer we got to 199B Vandam, the darker and colder and seedier everything became. Sort of picked up my spirits.

There was a black limo parked on a side street just down from the loft.

'Whose car is that?' Rambam asked.

'Garbage czar from New Jersey,' Ratso said.

'Vandam Street's a major garbage-truck staging area for the city,' I said, not without some little pride.

'I can see,' said Rambam, as he kicked his way through the swirling newspapers and crap along the sidewalk.

We drew a bye on the freight elevator and legged it up the stairs to the fourth floor. I opened the door of the loft, let Ratso and Rambam in ahead of me, and turned on the lights.

A thin dark man dressed in black was standing very still with his hand inside his coat. He looked like Johnny Cash in 1952. He looked dangerous. He was standing next to the hat rack, but it didn't look like he was planning to grab his hat and run.

There was another guy across the room from us standing by a window. He had a smile on his face but it was about as thin as airline coffee.

The rocking chair, which faced away from the door of the loft, was rocking slowly back and forth. It wouldn't have been so bad, except it didn't look like anybody was in it.

54

Somebody was.

A dark figure slowly uncoiled itself from the chair and stood up to face us. It moved toward us in silence. If Joel

Siegel had mated with Gene Shalit's daughter, and if their offspring had been a male child born with a luxuriant mustache, it might've looked similar to the cookie duster under the beak of the approaching apparition.

The figure came closer. Upon inspection, it had five shining emerald studs in its left ear. It had flat, dark, death-where-is-thy-sting eyes.

'I am the Jaguar,' it said.

There is almost nothing very humorous you can say in a situation like this. If raw courage is the ability not to let others know you are afraid, it could be said that I was very courageous. Because there was something about the presence of the Jaguar, despite his seemingly soft-spoken, refined manner, that transparently went against the grain of what it is to be human.

'You find the key I left for you?' I asked.

'The Jaguar doesn't use a key. For the Jaguar, there are no doors,' he said.

With a chill I thought about the story I'd read of a guy in Houston, a Colombian coke dealer, whom the cops had pinpointed, trapped, and tried to bust three times, only to find that he'd disappeared into thin air on each occasion. He was known as the Wizard, I believe. The Wizard. The Jaguar. There are many names for death, I thought.

Rambam moved up a few steps. He was still carrying the attaché case, but I figured by the time he could open it and take out the Uzi, we'd all be pickled herring.

My eyes flicked wistfully over to Rambam and the attaché case and then back to the Jaguar. The Jaguar continued to look straight ahead like a malicious Buddha.

'That won't be necessary, my friend,' he said. Then he paused and added, 'Or very effective.'

'Depends how you look at it,' said Rambam. He was holding what looked like some kind of high-tech police revolver in his right hand and aiming it placidly at the Jaguar's gonads.

I looked over my right shoulder and saw that Johnny Cash was now sporting a thin, gray cigar-box contraption with a long handle and a rather unpleasant-looking black nozzle extending from it. It was pointed at the back of my head and the guy was smiling.

It was an ugly situation at the very best. Rambam continued to look challengingly at the Jaguar. The Jaguar only licked his chops. I hazarded a side glance at Ratso. He did not look like a happy camper.

There were a couple other places I could think of that I'd rather be myself. Almost any of those bumper stickers that you always see would be fine. I'd rather be sailing. I'd rather be playing golf, though it bores me to death. The only good balls I ever hit was when I stepped on the garden rake. I'd rather be hang gliding.

Most of all, though, I'd rather be in a Jacuzzi one night many years ago under the stars of Malibu with the most beautiful girl in the world with a flower in her hair from Vancouver. The girl was from Vancouver, not the flower. I'd given her the flower. She wanted to make love in the Jacuzzi that night under the stars, but, coming from Texas, I was a bit inhibited. Today, of course, I'd hose her in a heartbeat, but that, unfortunately, would be quite impossible. She's wherever Dangerous Dan is, and I'm standing here in the loft with a man pointing an unusual-looking weapon at the back of my head and smiling like an airline stewardess.

I looked at the five shining emeralds in the Jaguar's ear and all I could think about was how much I missed the stars shining over Malibu. How much I missed somebody. How much I missed.

'Well?' said the Jaguar. He was smiling now, but the smile had all the humanity of an upside-down tragedy mask.

I looked at Johnny Cash. I looked at Rambam. I looked at the Jaguar.

'Colombian standoff?' I asked.

55

The Jaguar issued forth a thick, throaty, animal-like laugh and gave Johnny Cash a sign with his emerald-ringed finger. When I looked around, the weapon was back under Johnny Cash's coat and Johnny was still smiling, though not quite as much as when he'd thought he was going to get to use it. Rambam shook his head like a fireman who's seen too many false alarms and quietly slipped the gun back into a shoulder holster.

A little color was coming back into Ratso's face and he began, for the first time, to breathe perceptibly. I was starting to feel a little better myself.

I took out two cigars, offered one to the Jaguar, which he accepted, and then I walked over to the desk and guillotined the butt off my cigar in one rather decisive, macho movement. I motioned for the Jaguar to use the guillotine on his cigar. He shook his head and walked over to the kitchen table near where Ratso was standing.

From his breast pocket, the Jaguar took out a white object, gave it a dextrous flick, and walked close to Ratso with a bone-handled straight razor in his hand. Ratso looked like an extra from the cast of the movie *Coma*. He didn't turn a hair as the Jaguar moved past him, put the cigar on the table, and cut the end off like a master surgeon working with warm butter.

'Jesus,' Ratso said almost involuntarily. 'Do you shave with that?'

The guy by the far window said something in Spanish. The Jaguar and Johnny Cash both laughed.

'What'd he say?' I asked.

'He said,' said the Jaguar, 'if you shaved with it, you'd cut your lips off.'

It was pretty clear to me what the thing was used for, but as long as the Jaguar was slicing cigars and not working on passageways for lungs, it was okay by me.

'It is so sharp,' said the Jaguar, holding up the straight razor, 'that when you cut someone with it, they do not even know that they're cut for sometimes twenty seconds.' He folded the straight razor and put it back in his breast pocket.

'Sometimes,' I said, 'I bet they never find out.'

'That is true,' said the Jaguar. 'But that is only when the Jaguar wishes to be kind.'

The small talk had pretty well run its course. The Jaguar took out an expensive-looking gold lighter and lit his cigar. I took out the pastel-purple Bic I'd bought from the Pakistani the night I'd gone to Leila's apartment and met Carlos. If Bics could talk. That particular Bic had now seen two major cocaine-cartel kingpins, one very dead body in Estelle Beekman's closet, and one very live and lovely body when I'd lit a cigarette for Leila afterward. It had led a very exciting life for a Bic. Five days it had been with me and it was still going strong. That was longer than some marriages. Unfortunately, the lifespan of the Bic and my own mortality had in common a rather evanescent quality.

I lit the cigar. For a while the Jaguar and I stood around and quite literally blew smoke. Then he reached over and picked up a package from the seat of the rocking chair.

'It is good what you have done to Carlos,' he said, as he watched me closely. 'Carlos is no good. Carlos's people are no good. Did you receive the perla yi-yo?'

'Yes,' I said, 'but–'

The Jaguar silenced me with his hand. 'Here,' he said, 'is

136

another token of appreciation from the Jaguar. Some say it is even better than the perla yi-yo.'

Ratso rolled his eyes but didn't say anything. The Jaguar held the package out for me to take.

'Beware of geeks bearing gifts,' said Rambam in a stage whisper from my left.

I walked over to the Jaguar, thanked him, and took the package. He was one gift horse I wasn't even going to think about looking in the mouth. I carried the package over to the kitchen table. It was wrapped in the same butcher paper as the perla yi-yo. I tore off the paper.

If the Jaguar hadn't been a smarmy, evil, Freon-blooded killer, the gift would've been almost poignant.

'What is it?' Ratso asked. 'Heroin?'

'No,' I said, as I threw the package over the counter to Rambam, 'Coffee beans.'

Rambam went to work with the grinder and the espresso machine and pretty soon the loft was filled with an aroma so rich even my beezer could tell it was the McCoy. The whole place was threatening to become Kinky's Kosher Cajun Coffee Kitchen.

Suddenly, we heard the kitchen window break as if five or six baseballs had been thrown through it in extremely rapid succession. There was no other sound until Johnny Cash slumped to the floor. He was still smiling, but it looked like somebody'd crocheted his face.

Mustaches were moving along the fire escape.

It looked like it might be a while before anybody was going to have a cup of coffee.

56

The cat jumped over the moon, the Rat scurried for the hallway, and I ducked behind the kitchen counter. I could hear more invisible baseballs crashing through the windows, making no sound but for the breaking glass. I couldn't see Rambam. I couldn't see the Jaguar either, but I could imagine what he was thinking. Set up.

Then the lights went out. I glanced up and saw little cometlike tongues of fire coming through the windows. Wherever he was, it looked like the Jaguar had his hands full for the moment. It was a good thing, too, because the idea of the Jaguar stalking the Kinkster with a bone-handled straight razor in a darkened loft was enough to keep the sandman away for the rest of my life. Which, under the circumstances, might not be too long.

Strangely enough, I was not afraid. Or else I was so afraid that my fear had become a kind of quiet rage. If nothing else, I was determined to outlast the Bic.

I peered over the top of the counter into the semi-darkness. I saw several red flashes. A window crashed, and two mustaches bit the fire escape. But there were more, I suspected, where they came from. The Dixie cup kids.

There was a large crash from the direction of the bedroom that sounded like the wreck of the Hesperus. I took it to be the window that wouldn't open. I never said it *couldn't* be opened. I could see dim figures moving around in the bedroom. Men were shouting in Spanish. Strange sounds erupted like Paul Bunyan zipping and unzipping his fly many times in rapid succession. More figures crouched on the fire escape. The place sounded like a bullring with a rather small crowd. It looked like an urban Alamo.

Obviously, the Jaguar's boys were coming in from the west side of the building, and the other guys – who belonged to either Carlos or Santa Anna – were coming in from the front or south side. Directions can be important when you're lost in the woods in the dark. Without them, you might never get to Grandmother's house.

There was a strange aroma in the air – a heady, acrid, robust mixture of gunpowder and Colombian coffee. Very distinctive. You couldn't fool this crowd with Folger's crystals.

I didn't know how long I could stay there between the counter and the espresso machine before I caught a bullet, or realized twenty seconds too late that I'd been cut cleanly in half with a very sharp knife. I didn't want to be there, but everywhere else seemed worse.

Someone grabbed both my arms from the back in an iron grip. I looked around expecting to see a smiling mustache, and was somewhat relieved when I didn't. It was Rambam.

'Time to go,' he said. 'But stay down low.'

'Where to?' I asked.

He extended his hand toward the door of the loft like a maimtre d' showing me to a table.

'This way, Mr Kennedy,' he said, 'right through the kitchen.'

57

There is a rhythm to fear.

It's not something you pick up at Arthur Murray. It's measured in the statistical velocity at which the head and the feet can fly toward each other when the guts disappear. It's something you feel when you stand in a dark hallway and realize you may be about to die.

It has a sickly, draconic, not quite Caribbean flavor that can be very catchy when you see the cotton-candy-colored specter of death pressing its evil, childlike nose against the frosted glass of your mind. By then, of course, the party is o-v-e-r.

On the stairwell below I could hear the sound of a man dying in another language. I didn't plan to stick around for the translation. I was moving on up faster than the Jeffersons when Rambam caught me on the landing between the fourth and fifth floors. He had the Uzi on a strap around his neck. He handed me the police revolver.

'How do I use it?' I asked.

'You see anything that even faintly resembles a spic, you pull the trigger,' he said.

'Fine.' I didn't like this at all. Where the hell were the sirens? I wondered. I wanted sirens. I needed sirens.

'They're using MAC-10's with silencers,' said Rambam. 'That's the noise like a zipper you keep hearing.'

'Until they make contact,' I said. 'Then it sounds like somebody caught his shvantz in his Jordaches.'

'That gap-lapper with the dance class still up here?' asked Rambam as we hit the fifth floor.

'Yeah,' I said, as I looked at the pistol in my hand and at Rambam with his Uzi and Israeli Army jacket. 'But I'm not sure if she's ready for the raid on Entebbe.'

As we listened to the freight elevator creak ominously through the gloom, Rambam banged once on the door of Winnie Katz's loft, turned the knob, and threw it open.

If you're going to interrupt a lesbian dance class, you can't insist upon no surprises. We were ready for just about anything and that's just about what we got.

There was a Colombian lying barely inside the doorway. A bright red worm was crawling out of his head and moving in the general direction of the kitchen. Winnie Katz was standing over the body in a powder-blue warm-up suit, holding a MAC-10.

'How do you reload this cocksucker?' she asked.

There were sirens in the distance now, but I could see shadowy figures moving around on the fire escape. A fag in leotards came leaping by and two hysterical girls were cowering in the kitchen. Nothing wrong with cowering in the kitchen, I thought. I was just starting to look around the place when a barrage of shots forced us all to the floor and took out a large mirror on the wall behind us.

Rambam killed the lights, took up the Uzi, and cleared the fire escape, taking out every front window in the place. A quiet, uncertain moment followed in which everybody's ears rang and cold air and colder fear poured into the loft in about equal quantities. I looked outside but I didn't see any movement on the fire escape.

'You oughta get a silencer for that thing,' I said.

Rambam was looking out of one of the broken windows. 'Still a lot of action down there,' he said. 'I'll stay here. You check the bedroom.'

I walked across the darkened studio with my pistol out, like a gunfighter walking into the bar where the bad guys were. I didn't think anybody was in the bedroom, and I was pretty sure Rambam didn't either or he wouldn't've sent me in there. It was like sending seven different people to get blankets when you're treating a drowning victim. Gives everybody something to do, and maybe somebody shows up with a blanket in time to cover the guy before he dies of shock. If everybody shows up with blankets, you send them out again for beer and fried chicken and you have a picnic by the riverside.

Halfway to the bedroom I saw something move down by the floor under the desk. I crept closer and pointed the revolver in front of me. As I got very near the desk, a taut white face looked up at me. It was Ratso.

'What the hell are you doing?' I asked, dropping the gun to my side.

'What the fuck do you think I'm doing?' said Ratso. 'I'm calling 911!'

'Jesus Christ, Ratso, how long does it take to call 911?'

'I'm on hold,' he said.

I walked over to the bedroom, prepared to take a quick, cursory look around. I walked in about four or five nervous steps. There wasn't even a bed in the place, just one of those tofu mattresses. Lesbians are weird, all right.

As I turned to leave the room, a figure suddenly detached itself from the far wall and flew at me like a desperate bat. It was too dim in the room to tell if it faintly resembled a spic, but it had a long, shiny knife in one hand so I pulled the trigger. The knife seemed to flutter against my throat like a steel moth and then it fell away. At that distance, with Rambam's big gun, even Mr Magoo would've been deadly. The bat bit the tofu.

I hit the lights and looked at the body. It was very dead. The first life I'd ever taken. A line came into my head from the poet Kenneth Patchen: 'There are so many little dyings, it doesn't matter which of them is death.' I turned the body over with my foot.

It was Carlos.

I stood there for a moment breathing like the guy who came in 791st in the Boston Marathon.

'Call your sister,' I said.

58

I crept back across the studio like an anxious crab. Rambam was peering out of the doorway into the hall and motioned me to join him. Two dark figures had forced the doors of the freight elevator, and a third was firing down into the shaft with a MAC-10. The wall switch for the elevator had been thrown and apparently it had stopped between floors. There was no roof to the freight elevator; it was little more than a grimy cage with a light bulb hanging from two crossbars. It was like shooting fish in a barrel, except that the fish were screaming and cursing in Spanish, and the racket was echoing in the elevator shaft.

It sounded, to quote my pal Tom Waits, 'like Jerry Lewis going down on the *Titanic*.'

After the fish began to sound more like ceviche, the three figures turned from the elevator and Rambam field-stripped them with the Uzi. He stepped over the bodies, threw the switch, and pushed the down button, which sent the stiffs in the elevator to the ground floor.

'Lingerie,' he said.

We could hear cops in the hallway now and random shots being fired in the street. We went back into Winnie's place and collected Ratso.

Winnie seemed calm and cool. 'You want some Red Zinger tea?' she asked.

'No thanks,' I said. 'I've got some coffee downstairs.'

Rambam casually gave his Uzi to the dead Colombian by the doorway.

'Illegal,' he whispered to me.

'I see,' I said. I gave the revolver back to him.

By the time Rambam, Ratso, and I got back to the loft, the cops were swarming all over the place. There were more crushed Colombian Dixie cups lying around than I'd thought, but, like Rambam said, they were expendable.

I conducted a rather agonizing search for my cat, finally locating her in the closet in the bedroom. She was fine. Just a little pissed off. I gave her some tuna.

I took out about forty-nine cups and poured coffee for anyone who wanted it. I guessed that it would be a long, tedious debriefing, or whatever they called it, and I was right.

I got myself a cup of coffee and walked through the loft surveying the damage. It didn't look too bad. Of course, it hadn't looked too good to begin with.

I was able to observe only one casualty on our side: The puppet head had taken a direct hit.

There was one other thing I noticed that bothered me almost as much as the loss of the puppet head.

There was no sign of the Jaguar.

59

Two days later, on a crisp, cold Tuesday morning, I was having breakfast with Eugene in the little Greek coffee shop at the rather obscene hour of 8 a.m. I had asked for the meeting, not the other way around. I wanted to get this Rocky-Goldberg-Estelle Beekman situation spanked and put to bed. The sooner the better. Eight o'clock in the morning was a little early for my blood, but some people work for a living and Eugene was one of them. I wanted to meet with him away from the publishing house.

'Eugene,' I said, 'I need your help.'

'What can I do?' he asked.

You can stop wearing that yellow knit tie, I thought. I sipped a hot cup of coffee and mulled it over. 'I need someone,' I said, 'on the inside, so to speak. Someone more familiar with the publishing business than I am.'

'Why don't you talk to Jim or Jane?'

'I'm going to talk to everybody, but Landis is being unco-operative and Jane is the one I'm worried about.'

'I'm worried about her, too,' said Eugene. 'I gave her a manuscript over a month ago and she hasn't finished it yet. That's not like her.'

'What was the manuscript?'

'A novel I wrote.'

'No kiddin'? What kind of novel?'

'It doesn't matter,' he said. 'Nobody's ever going to find

144

out, the way things are going. If Hemingway were around today he'd probably be writing ad copy.'

'You're right,' I said. And he was. Van Gogh had been able to sell only one painting in his lifetime. The painting was *The Red Harvest* and he sold it to his brother, Theo. Good ol' Theo. Franz Schubert's estate at the time of his death was valued at twelve cents. He didn't have a brother around to buy the *Unfinished* Symphony.

'It's frustrating,' said Eugene. 'Jane's just got to come to grips with reality. She's got to realize that that cat is *gone*. It's not just affecting her work – it's affecting her mind.'

'Yeah,' I said. It was affecting my mind, too.

Eugene did not know Goldberg. Eugene did not know Estelle Beekman. Eugene had to get to work. Fine.

If Eugene had not been my ideal choice for a breakfast companion, Hilton Head for brunch was worse. I had to talk to these people. The battle of the Colombian drug cartels on Sunday night had convinced me that the Kukulcán angle, the possibility that the Colombians were behind Goldberg's and Estelle Beekman's demises for some reason that was connected with Jane Meara's cat, was very doubtful to say the least. Men who kill with silenced MAC-10's, who perform Colombian neckties, who perform Colombian butterflies, would be more creatively cruel and clever than merely to cut a man's tongue out. And it had been a sloppy job at that. I didn't see the mark of the Jaguar there, so to speak. But who knew?

Sunday night had also convinced me that the Baby Jesus wanted me to love for some reason. To save Jane's life? To find Rocky? I didn't know, but I doubted if the reason was so that I could have brunch with Hilton Head.

I had brunch with Head in the Village. Wanted him to

feel he belonged. We ate at some chic European rabbit-food place that blew in more ways than one.

I browbeat Head about what Leila was doing coming and going from his apartment. Finally, he told me.

'Just delivering a little shmutz,' he said, He pronounced it like 'fruits.'

'Shmutz?'

'Cocaine,' he whispered irritably.

'Oh, yeah,' I said. 'Shmutz.'

It was not uncommon, I'd learned, for people to give harmless little names to very deadly, dangerous things. Ted Mann had once told me about an heiress he'd known, from some spiritually bankrupt family, who also called cocaine shmutz. She'd snort about eight grams a day and drink about four bottles of vodka. She'd destroyed her mind entirely and her very life was hanging on a thread and here she was still calling it shmutz. 'I'll just have a little shmutz.' Well, we all have our blind spots.

The only other interesting thing that emerged from the Head brunch was that Hilton, several years before he'd come out of the closet, had dated Estelle Beekman for a while. He didn't seem in great grief about her death. He seemed more to think it was rather pathetic.

I wasn't a professional checkup-from-the-neck-up kind of guy. Just your normal dime-store Jungian. But I really thought Head's sexual evolution let him off the hook. I couldn't see a guy who'd finally come out of the closet ever wanting to put somebody else back into it.

60

I had lunch back at the loft with Ratso and the cat. I'd already had two meals, if you wanted to call them that, and I was still hungry enough to eat a tofu mattress.

Ratso and I ordered in from a Nip place he wanted to try. Several hours later it nipped us back pretty good. It was a meal that would live in infamy.

The cat had tuna.

Ratso and I used chopsticks. The cat did not.

I'd always felt that the Chinese were smarter than the Japanese, and one of the arguments that I frequently used to support this thesis was that they ate Chinese food instead of Japanese food.

'So how'd it go with Hilton?' Ratso asked, affecting a slight lisp.

I told him.

'Could be some clues there,' he said.

'Your rather obsessional quest for what you call clues, my dear Ratso, can sometimes be counterproductive, not to mention tedious. What we must ask ourselves is this: If Jane Meara is the killer's next intended victim – and I, for one, believe she is – what does that tell us? What kind of pattern presents itself?'

'Yeah,' said Ratso, 'but what about Estelle and Head having an affair? What about your friend Leila running cocaine to Head? What about the discrepancy over whether or not Stanley Park ever visited Jane's office that day?'

'Pace yourself,' I said. 'These things, I think you'll find, are what we in the business of detection commonly refer to as red herrings.'

'I've heard the term,' said Ratso in a somewhat miffed tone. 'What about the possible involvement of the Colombians, though? What about Carlos?'

'That's a dead herring,' I said. 'Ratso, when this case is solved, I don't think the killer will be a Colombian. It'll most likely be a normal American just like you or me. It'll probably be an average member of the white larval middle class. Of course, we may, in a deeper sense, never

147

find the killer. There are those of us who feel that life itself may be a red herring.'

'Let's not get too metaphysical,' said Ratso. I poured us each a cup of the finest Colombian coffee in the world.

'Is perla yi-yo,' I said. 'Speaking of which, where the hell's the other perla yi-yo?'

'I'll make you a deal,' said Ratso. 'You solve the case by the weekend, I'll tell you where in the loft I hid the perla yi-yo.'

'You're not asking for much, are you?'

'Is it a deal?'

I took another sip of Colombian coffee. I shook Ratso's hand grimly.

It didn't give me a hell of a lot of time. Of course, I didn't *have* to solve the damn thing by the weekend. But it would be nice.

61

'It's nothing,' I said. 'I've just got this special knack for being in the wrong place at the wrong time.'

Jane Meara and an attractive friend of hers, Lori Ames, were both cooing over a McGovern bylined article on page 1 of the *Daily News*. It was part two of a multipart series about how a country singer who was a close personal friend of the journalist had almost single-handedly brought about the downfall of two of the largest Colombian cocaine cartels operating in the city.

'You're hot shit,' said Lori Ames.

'Thank you,' I said.

We were sitting in a restaurant on Mulberry Street in Little Italy. It was late Tuesday afternoon and I was eating lightly. Sending some Wop food down to try to straighten out the little eruption by the pesky Nips. Or maybe it was the brunch with Hilton Head that had done it. Normally, I could eat anything without getting upset. I thought of Leila. She hadn't called in several days now. Never trust a Palestinian.

The restaurant the three of us were in was called Luna's and was one of the best in Little Italy. It was run by a woman named Yola and I can't remember how many times I'd seen Ratso, on very crowded nights, walk up to the front of a long line of people waiting to get in, and wave to Yola. She'd come over and get us a table right away. The people would mutter while we spread bread with butter.

Luna's was also the last place Ratso and I had had dinner with our friend Mike Bloomfield, the great blues guitarist, before he died. It was also where he'd once taken my friend Dennis McKenna, who on that occasion had been a very drunken Irishman. When the *capo* of one of the city's major crime families had suddenly appeared, wearing vaguely sinister Old World garb, the whole place had gone silent. That was when McKenna had called out to the man, 'Nice hat!'

'The ASPCA has been very helpful,' said Jane Meara.

'What?' I said.

'In trying to locate Rocky.'

'Yeah,' I said. 'If there's a way to run her down, they ought to know it. Pardon the expression.'

'You don't think we'll find her, do you?' asked Jane.

'I think we'll find out where Rocky is when we find the killer. We could find the killer by this weekend,' I said. Of course, Dallas could melt by this weekend.

'Jane,' I said, 'why haven't you read Eugene's manuscript?'

'Oh, he told you, did he? That little brat. He's bugging me to death about it. I'll read it when I find out about Rocky.'

'You may find out something you don't want to,' I said. I thought of how Rocky might look dying in an alley, the victim of a Colombian butterfly.

'I'll take my chances,' said Jane.

Lori Ames had been reading the *Daily News* piece while Jane and I had been yapping. Now she looked up at me and, shucking all modesty, there was admiration in her eyes.

'You know something?' she said.

'What?'

'You're hot shit.'

'Don't put me up on a pedestal,' I said.

I'd been on the human rodeo circuit long enough to know that you couldn't change people's minds by telling them the truth. If McGovern's articles had half of New York believing I was a hero who'd cleverly and courageously contrived to bring two major drug cartels to their knees, who was I to say it wasn't true? If I'd told Lori Ames the truth of how I'd stumbled into the whole mess, she probably wouldn't've believed me anyway. So I might as well enjoy the ride.

As the three of us left Luna's, something Sherlock Holmes once said came into my mind. Sherlock was explaining to Watson his hesitance to reveal his methods, because once he'd done so, he'd in effect demystified himself. When he revealed his methodology to his clients, they tended to be somewhat blaseк about the results. They said things like 'Oh, I could've told you that.'

What Sherlock actually said to Watson was 'What you do in this world is a matter of no consequence. The question is, what can you make people think you have done?'

As the weekend grew ever closer, I'd probably have to borrow a page from Sherlock. If things got really rough, I thought, maybe I'd lift the whole book.

62

As it evolved, I borrowed a page from Nero Wolfe before I borrowed a page from Sherlock. It was like borrowing a cup of sugar from a yesterday that never was, but if certain things had worked for Sherlock and Mr Wolfe, why not for the Kinkster? Indeed.

The problem was that I was not a fictional person and I was not dealing with fictional people. When you work with flesh and blood, as God probably found out on day eight, things tend to break down a little. In real life, Cinderella tires of the prince and has an affair with the boy who comes to clean the swimming pool. In real life, Sleeping Beauty has insomnia. Of course, on the other hand, the Village was one of the few places, outside of certain dense forests in Ireland, where fairies could still often be seen. Sometimes they'd even grant you a wish. Like get out of your way so you could park your car.

Late Tuesday night, after a couple of shots of Jameson, I told Ratso my plan. He was somewhat skeptical, but every Jesus needs a Doubting Thomas to sort of keep him on his toes. Not that I thought I was Jesus, of course. I was having enough trouble with Sherlock Holmes and Nero Wolfe.

'Here's the plan,' I told Ratso. 'Thursday night at eight o'clock we invite all the principals in the case here to the loft. The Parks, Head, Jane, Landis, Eugene, and maybe a special guest or two. We'll also have Cooperman here. We'll have Peter Myers cater the affair. You with me so far?'

'Sure,' said Ratso. 'It's the only invitation I've gotten all week.'

'Okay, now we get these people over here–'

'What if they don't come?'

'Oh, they'll come all right. Not showing up would amount to a tacit confession of guilt. Besides, who the hell are they?

George Jones? Greta Garbo? Of course they'll show. They wouldn't dare *not* show. Anyway, when they get here, in the manner of Nero Wolfe we sit them all down, serve food and drinks, and then, with a little incisive probing and a little normal human interaction, we'll get some interesting results.

'Now, I've got some work to do myself tomorrow, so I'd appreciate it if you'd call the list and get the whole thing set up.'

'You're out of your mind,' said Ratso. 'You can call me a homosexual pancake chef, but I'll be damned if I'll be your male social secretary.'

'You can't very well expect Nero Wolfe himself to make the calls. Our guests would find it highly unsatisfactory, not to mention rather gauche. This is really quite juvenile, Archie.'

'Archie? Who the hell's Archie?'

'Archie Goodwin,' I said patiently, 'was Nero Wolfe's assistant. If you read anything other than books relating to Jesus, Bob Dylan, and Hitler, you'd've known that.'

'God,' said Ratso, 'what a horrible cultural gap in my very being. All because I didn't read a certain dime-novel whodunit.'

'It is the kind of gap,' I said, 'through which a clever killer can sometimes escape.'

I poured a healthy shot of Jameson and puffed on a cigar. Ratso walked over to the door of the loft and bolted it.

'Why are you doing that?' I asked.

'Well, Mr Wolfe, you forget that there's a Jaguar out there somewhere and he's familiar with this address.'

'Ah, but Archie, you know that for the Jaguar there are no doors.'

'I know that,' said Ratso, 'but we don't have to make it a fucking cakewalk for him.'

I killed the shot. I killed the light. I killed the temptation to say something to Ratso. I walked into the bedroom, put on my sarong, and went to bed. As luck would have it, I did not dream.

63

Wednesday morning while Ratso slept, I ran a routine search for the perla-yi-yo, just in case I didn't find the killer by the weekend. I didn't know what I'd do with that much cocaine if I found it. I wasn't even sure I wanted any amount of cocaine. But I knew it was there somewhere in the loft. It was kind of like finding the *afikomen*.

I didn't find anything but an old letter I never sent to a broad I never really got to know. Nothing lost. A lot of things in life fall behind dressers and get lost in the cobwebs and we don't even know the difference. Of course, there's a lot of hip spiders walking around somewhere.

At 10 a.m., the time all good agents should be in their offices, I lifted the blower on the left and posted a call to Lobster.

I wanted Lobster to rifle Slick Goldberg's files personally. Both those on his current clients, if you wanted to call them that, and his reject-letter files. Slick had worked for a large agency where, as was the rule, nobody really knew what anybody else was doing. Lobster's job was to get into his office on any pretense, even that of seeing another agent, and finding the goods. Also, I requested that she worm her way into Estelle Beekman's old publishing house and check those files as well. I told her what to look for and that I needed it by the weekend.

'I'm going to do this for you just this one time,' said Lobster. 'I don't really know why.'

'Maybe it's my rural charm,' I said.

I left the Nero Wolfe party list on the desk where Ratso would be sure to see it, and I went out to lunch. I dined at a swank and fairly unpronounceable French restaurant on the Upper East Side where I had to take my hat off to get in.

Normally, I wouldn't have stood for that, but then, normally I didn't have lunch with Fred Katz.

64

Wednesday night I stayed up late with the cat and what was left of the bottle of Jameson. Ratso, having called the list and ordered a roast and two dozen pork pies from Pete Myers, had gone to play hockey. I sat at the desk. The cat and the bottle sat on the desk between the two red telephones to keep me company. I wasn't an alcoholic. Alcoholics drink alone.

I was reading a clipping a friend had sent to me several weeks before. It wasn't related to the case at hand. Well, let's say it wasn't directly related to the case at hand. The article looked like it was from the *New York Post* or the *National Enquirer*, the kind of paper that occasionally has the guts to print things that are not fit to print.

The source of the article was *The Compendium on Continuing Education for the Practicing Veterinarian*. The part of it that jumped out at me was a statement to the effect that '57 percent of cat owners confide in their cats about important matters.'

'What in the hell,' I said to the cat, 'have I gotten myself into?'

The cat didn't say anything. I downed a shot of Jameson from the old bull's horn.

'What in the hell,' I said to the cat, 'am I going to do if nothing happens tomorrow night?'

The cat demurred. I poured and killed another shot.

'And what do you think of Ratso?' I asked. 'In his own stubborn, neurotic, New York way, he believes in me. His loyalty is almost poignant, don't you think? Kind of like a gynecologist daydreaming of his wife . . .'

The cat licked her paw a few times and closed her eyes. I wondered what percentage of cats gave a shit about the confidences of their owners.

I knocked back another fairly stiff one.

'Nice of you to listen to all of this,' I said rather facetiously.

The cat yawned. I poured another shot.

'The way I see it,' I said, 'we've been looking in the wrong places for the wrong things. We've misconducted the case in the same manner that most of us misconduct our lives. Of course, this time we've had more than our share of red herrings and blind alleys, but still, there's no excuse. I think I see the solution. And it's really very simple. The problem is going to be how to prove it without somebody punching Jane Meara's dance card for the river Styx.

'Look at it this way. What strategy would Tom Landry, the coach of my second favorite team, the Dallas Cowboys, have used if he were alive today? Are you listenin'?'

The cat was sitting with her back to me, which was something she occasionally did when a person or a situation greatly displeased her.

I ignored this rude behavior.

'Maybe I should've been a Buddhist or a dusty old Navajo. Maybe everything would seem clearer then. I just don't understand people today. There's a sign on the highway near our ranch in Texas that says 'Waterfall for Sale.' You ever hear of anything like that? Guy thinks he can sell a waterfall. Hell, maybe he can. You in the market for slightly used waterfalls? How about a guy who never quite made it to the top as a country singer so he tries his hand at something much more difficult and deadly?

Sometimes it looks like a guitar picker just can't tell what to pick. He rambles around the world until he suddenly stumbles head first into a situation that makes him a hero with feet of Play-Do.

'If I'm wrong tomorrow night, well . . . we can go on the road again. You and me and the old guitar and the pillow-case. You never did like traveling in a pillowcase much, but who said life on the road was gonna be easy? A middle-aged misanthrope and his cat playing county fairs and rodeos . . .'

I killed the last shot. I looked at the cat. The cat was sound asleep. By the time Ratso got back from his hockey game, I was, too.

65

Thursday night rolled around like a battered beach ball. The loft, however, looked like a million bucks. Two rows of mismatched furniture, including folding chairs, the rocker, and a hassock that appeared to be left over from *The Adventures of Ozzie & Harriet*, were arranged neatly in front of my desk. Nero Wolfe would've been proud.

The windows sparkled. That was because they were new windows, put in to replace the ones blown away by Rambam and the boys from Brazil or wherever the hell they came from.

I was wearing my formal black Italian tuxedo jacket, which had once belonged to a Puerto Rican coke dealer. A little class never hurt anything.

Pete Myers was standing in the kitchen with a long knife, cutting what looked like an obscenely large portion of a farm animal into paper-thin slices. Pork pies from his shop on Hudson Street were laid out all along the counter with hot mustard, chutney, and a few other things I didn't recognize. Also, there were several large bottles of the ever-present HP sauce. I thought, but did not verbalize, the sentiment that a famous frog had once expressed: 'In England there are sixty different religions, and only one sauce.' It would've been in questionable taste.

'These friends of yours coming tonight, Kinkster?' asked Myers in his soft, northern English Lake District accent.

''Fraid not,' I said.

'One of 'em's a murderer,' said Ratso in his rather rodent-like, grating Queens accent. 'Tonight Kinky's gonna unmask the fiend. Right, Kinkster?'

'Right,' I said a little shakily as I reached for a bottle of Guinness.

'Pour enough of that stuff down your neck and you may unmask yourself,' said Myers.

'Wouldn't be the first time,' said Ratso.

'Right,' I said with a measure of dignity.

I took the Guinness and walked over to the kitchen window. With the puppet head out of commission, Ratso and I were going to have to do a lot of legwork going down to the front door each time to let the guests in. Of course, if you want to entertain, you have to be prepared to make sacrifices. I poured a little Guinness down my neck and looked out at the empty street. What if Nero Wolfe gave a party, I thought, and nobody came?

By ten-thirty only two pork pies and two detective sergeants were still hanging around. The two detective sergeants were leaving and Ratso was putting the two pork pies into the refrigerator.

'See you around, hero,' said Cooperman.

'Call us when you get another bright idea like this,' said Fox. I let them out the door, poured another Guinness down my neck, and sat down at the desk facing two little rows of disheveled, empty furniture.

Everyone had come and everyone had gone, and now everything was quiet except for a little garbage-truck activity starting up on Vandam Street. Like someone going over the minutes of a past Rotarian meeting, I ticked off the high points of the evening in my mind. During the course of the little affair I'd also managed to tick off some of my guests, but that can't always be helped. Being a society host is not my long suit.

Jim Landis had shown up about half an hour late. As a result, he'd had to sit on the *Ozzie & Harriet* hassock and he wasn't any too happy about it. Something else was eating him, too, but whatever it was, he didn't want to share it with the whole class. Relations between Jim and Jane, and Jim and Eugene, seemed rather strained. Some internal politics were going on that did not look very pleasant, but what they were was anybody's guess.

Jane and Eugene, for their part, said very little, though leading questions were asked and touchy subjects and confrontations were common during the course of the evening.

When I asked Eugene if the Parks and Hilton Head were the three people he'd seen up in the office the day the butcher knife was found on Jane's desk, he said yes to Marilyn Park and Hilton Head and no to Stanley Park. Who was the third person? I asked. No reply.

Stanley Park became slightly *agitato*. In fact, the ugliness became so thick you could've cut it with a knife.

Finally, Head cleared the air. The third person had been his 'friend.' Who was the friend? He'd rather keep the friend out of it.

I let it pass. The friend was out of it anyway. It was something the Parks could squabble over, or Head could fret over, on their own time.

Everyone was alert to questions regarding Estelle

Beekman or Slick Goldberg. Many of them had probably read Nero Wolfe, too.

I was creative, clever, crude, caustic, conciliatory, conniving, and just about everything else that starts with a *c*, but none of them snapped their wigs and ran madly for the door into the waiting arms of Sergeant Cooperman. Everybody played it cool. Everybody had alibis for the times when Goldberg and Beekman had gotten aced.

It was quite a three-cigar problem. I watched for hands tensing, facial muscles twitching, other signs of noticeable discomfort, but it was hard to watch seven Americans at once. I learned little that I didn't already know.

The only one in the room who seemed to be legitimately socializing was the cat. She turned her back on Marilyn Park's advances and walked over to sniff at Jane Beara's boots.

'Kinky's cat has a leather fetish,' said Head. Landis chuckled. Most of the group, being cat fanciers, found little humor in the remark.

The cat walked over to Eugene and leaped into his lap. He tried to push her away, but if you've ever tried to push away a cat who doesn't want to go away, you know it can't be done. She preened herself, rubbed up against him, and pawed at his stomach in a friendly cat manner. Eugene, though obviously a bit stiff and uncomfortable about this sudden feline attention, held up pretty well under the circumstances.

'Enjoy it, pal,' said Cooperman. 'It may be the only pussy you'll get tonight.' Fox laughed. Marilyn Park pursed her lips in a little moue of distaste.

Just as the natives were starting to get restless, I introduced Fred Katz to the group for the first time by name. This brought about the strongest reaction of the night. Many in the small group were convinced from my *Daily News* advertisement and from talk they had heard that Fred Katz was the villain of the piece. I observed reactions carefully. Jane looked horrified. Nobody grabbed him by the throat, but Stanley Park and Eugene were both on their feet in outrage. The cat went flying. She rubbed herself against my leg in an effort to regain her dignity.

I hushed the crowd. They returned to their seats. 'Fred Katz is no cat-napper,' I said. 'Nor is he a murderer.' The crowd oohed and ahhed a bit. I puffed on cigar number three.

'Fred Katz is a financial consultant, which, in some quarters, might be regarded as equally odious. But, for our purposes, he is innocent. The only thing he's guilty of is checking out and leaving his key in his hotel room.'

The cat jumped back into Eugene's lap. Eugene took the ordeal rather stoically this time. Cooperman leaned his mug into the group and said, 'Hey, buddy, at least get her phone number.'

Jim Landis announced he'd 'had enough of this charade' and he was leaving. Others got up to go. Some said thanks and good night. Some just beat it out the door. I poured another Guinness down my neck.

At the door, I hugged Jane Meara and whispered to her to be careful, we were getting close. She looked at me like I was an outpatient.

Now I gazed across the tiny ocean of empty chairs and puffed languidly on what was left of cigar number three. Ratso came over and slumped down across from me in the rocker. He looked at my face closely, almost sadly.

'Looks like a washout, Mr Wolfe,' he said.

'Quite to the contrary, my dear Ratso,' I said. 'Quite to the contrary.'

Early Friday afternoon, while I was waiting around for Lobster to call, I made the mistake of telling Ratso about my joshman dream. Now, as he walked back into the room wearing his hockey kneepads, I began to wonder about the wisdom of my disclosure.

'There's nothing wrong with being a latent homosexual,' said Ratso, as he adjusted his kneepads and walked over to the refrigerator.

'I'm not one,' I said curtly. 'It's just . . . the gentler, more sensitive side of me manifesting itself. The actual dream definition of joshman means nothing. It just reflects a longing.'

'Tell that to Hilton Head,' said Ratso. 'I'm sure he's quite an authority on joshman.'

'Forget it,' I said. 'It was just a dream.'

'I wouldn't worry about it none,' said Ratso, as he took a pork pie out of the refrigerator. 'Them ol' dreams are only in your head.' He closed the refrigerator door. 'Bob Dylan,' he said.

'That's an unusual source for you to quote from,' I said.

'Beats Rita Mae Brown.'

The phones rang. It was 1.15 p.m. It was Lobster and she had the goods. It was just as I expected. I put down the blower and allowed myself a deep sigh of relief. I took a cigar from Sherlock's head and lopped the butt off it with the guillotine.

Then I called Jim Landis.

Fortunately, he wasn't at lunch or at a sales conference, the two places where people like him seemed to spend most of their lives. Unfortunately, he didn't want to speak to me.

'This is matter,' I told the secretary, 'of life or death.' I was put on hold.

I made a cup of espresso and found and put on my brontosaurus foreskin boots while I waited. What you do with the hold time in your life is an index of how successful you'll be when your call finally comes through. A wise old judge told me he'd once heard of a Jew, an Italian, and a person of the Polish persuasion who all had been sentenced to twenty years in prison for bank robbery. The Jew had wanted a telephone, the Italian had requested conjugal rights, and the Polish individual had demanded four hundred cartons of cigarettes in his cell. Twenty years later, the Jew had built a worldwide corporate empire, the Italian left prison with a family of eight, and the person of the Polish persuasion came out of his cell with an unlit cigarette dangling from his lip and said, 'Got a match?'

At least I had a match. I lit the cigar. The secretary came back on the line.

'Mr Landis wants to know *whose* life or death,' she said.

'Tell him *his* life or death,' I said with some intensity. 'If he doesn't pick up the phone right now, I'll call a hit on him by the Jewish Defense League. And don't think I can't.'

This is the kind of thing you get used to when you're dealing with professional people in general. They have their lives just a little out of perspective and sometimes you have to tell them what is important and what isn't. You have to be aggressive.

'Yes, Kinky?' Landis said like a patronizing aunt.

'Where's Jane?'

'Out,' he answered brusquely.

'Sorry about last night,' I said. 'You don't like charades?'

'Only with eccentric, best-selling British mystery writers in drafty old manor houses.'

'I can see how you'd be disappointed,' I said, 'but the little charade had its little purposes. You see, it helped me identify the killer.'

Landis didn't say anything. I took a puff on the cigar and looked over at Ratso. He was sitting across the room on the couch with the screwdriver in his hand. He'd been ready to turn on the television, but my last sentence apparently had gotten his attention. Now he looked over at me. I nodded to him.

'Jim,' I said, 'tell me about this manuscript that Eugene supposedly has given Jane and that Jane supposedly's been squirreling away, threatening to read for over a month.'

'Oh, that,' laughed Landis. 'I looked at it once briefly when it was lying on Jane's desk. Eugene's masterpiece.'

'What was it about?'

'It was a book about dogs,' said Landis lightly. 'The *Jonathan Livingston Seagull* of dog books.'

'That tears it,' I said grimly. 'Jim, this is important. *Where is Jane*?'

'She's been acting a little spooked lately, so I let her take the afternoon off. I think she went to the circus at Madison Square Garden. Maybe she thinks she'll find her cat. Is anything wrong?'

'Yeah,' I said.

I got my coat and two cigars for the road and walked over to Ratso. I looked at the overly large hockey kneepads he was still wearing.

'Either take those fucking things off or put on the rest of the uniform. And hurry.'

'Where we goin'?' he asked.

'Back to the Garden,' I said. 'The circus is in town in more ways than one.'

67

There is a time to live and a time to die and a time to stop listening to albums by the Byrds. Now, as we hurtled uptown toward the Garden at high speed in a hack that rattled like a child's toy, I only prayed that my unorthodox assemblage of what Ratso still rather archaically referred to as clues was correct.

I thought of the last phone call I'd made just before we'd left the loft. It had been to Sergeant Cooperman and it had made the previous call to Jim Landis seem like spun cotton candy.

Heroes, it seemed, had a rather short wingspan in New York. Either that, or Cooperman did not believe what he read in the *Daily News*. I felt like Sly Stone's lawyer. When Sly had suddenly found his house surrounded by police cars, he'd called the lawyer and reportedly said, 'You get over here now. And you better be heavy and you better be white.'

Being white is an accident of birth. Being heavy is spiritually relative. What I had to be, in no uncertain terms, according to Sergeant Cooperman, was right. And right is sometimes the hardest thing to be in the world.

As we stepped out of the hack and into the throng, I wondered, not for the first time, if I could be making a terrible mistake. It was the kind of case where logical deduction hardly followed logical deduction. Philip Marlowe, with his dogged perseverance, would've had a better shot at cracking it than Hercule Poirot, with his little gray cells. I'd started looking for a cat, stumbled across two stiffs along the way, gotten shot by a lion tranquilizer dart, been sidetracked by a Jaguar, and now, with any luck, I was finally closing in on the killer.

Train schedules and comments by the butler were not going to catch a murderer in 1988 in America. We'd been to the movies. We'd grown up on television. And to make things even harder, in the words of Mark Twain: 'There is no distinctly native American criminal class except Congress.'

And yet, when I went over it again in my mind, I was sure I had it right. Like Inspector Maigret, walking the rainy streets of Paris, smoking my pipe, my hands in my pockets, watching the people caught up in the problems of their lives, I would solve this case. After all, like Maigret, I was a serious student of human nature. And, come to think of it, not-so-human nature.

I didn't see Cooperman or Fox in the foyer, but there wasn't a hell of a lot of time to waste, so I gave Ratso forty bucks, told him to buy two tickets, and then I went over and talked to a uniform who was picking his nose near the doorway. I told him Detective Sergeants Cooperman and Fox from the Sixth Precinct were on their way, and I told him the vicinity where I thought Ratso and I would be. That was the best I could do under the circumstances.

Ratso returned with the tickets. I don't know what circus tickets cost these days, but I didn't see any change. Maybe Ratso threw in a service charge.

We went in.

Going to the circus as an adult is not the same as going to the circus as a child. The difference is, when you're an adult, all the clowns tend to look like John Wayne Gacy.

It was now pushing two o'clock, when the show was supposed to start. Martha Hume, a sassy, southern, circus-going friend of mine, had told me some time ago that there are holding cages in the basement where you can see the animals up close before the circus starts. The place is called the menagerie, and if I was right, I thought, as we headed down the Dantean ramps into the noisy bowels of the Garden, it would certainly be one today. If I was wrong, Jane could be sitting in the third row eating peanuts and watching normally rational animals making fools of themselves for other animals who already were fools. Life's a circus, or it's a carnival, or a whorehouse, or a wishing well. Or a winding, muddy river. One of those things. About the only thing we know life isn't is a Norman Rockwell painting. But don't tell your dentist that. Dentists have their dreams.

We were coming to the end of the last ramp, and the suspicion I held was getting stronger as we progressed downward. Evil has its logic, I thought. Mental illness has its patterns. I was betting Jane's life that I had accurately gazed into the mind of a maniac.

I hoped Cooperman and Fox would show up soon. If not, it looked like Ratso and I were going to be working without a net.

68

'Looks like it's closed and we're hosed,' said Ratso, as we tried vainly to open the two locked doors at the end of the ramp.

'Think, Ratso,' I said. 'You're a pro at getting backstage at rock concerts. What do we do?'

'I'll tell Dumbo the Elephant that I know Ron Wood,' said Ratso.

I banged loudly on the metal doors. Nothing. It was two o'clock. Upstairs, we could hear the grand parade kicking off. There had to be somebody around. I kept pounding the doors.

Finally, an old man with a funny hat opened the doors. It could be said that Ratso and I were wearing funny hats, too, but we were wearing very serious faces.

'Detective Sergeant Cooperman,' I said. 'Sixth Precinct. Undercover.' I flashed the idiot button inside my wallet at him. It was a courtesy badge that had been given to me by Lieutenant Scott Grabin of the NYPD, one of the few cops on the force I still enjoyed good relations with. That was because I rarely saw Grabin. He worked out of a precinct in Harlem. Maybe if somebody burned a watermelon in my front yard we'd have the opportunity to work on a case together.

'This is Sergeant Fox,' I said quickly, nodding toward Ratso. 'We're looking for a small boy who's on special heart medication. Been missing for over an hour. We're runnin' out of time.'

The only other occasion on which I'd ever used the idiot button was when I'd gotten drunk once in a Mexican restaurant and tried to arrest some of the patrons. It hadn't worked then and it didn't look like it was going to work now.

Then Ratso, drawing heavily on his New York background, pushed the old man to the side and shouted authoritatively, 'C'mon, gramps! Get out of the way!' The old man did. Ratso and I walked purposefully through a length of empty corridor and started searching around. We didn't look back.

'Not especially kind,' I said.

'It gets results, Sergeant.'

We turned a corner and entered what seemed like a large, dank, dark hall. The circus music coming through the ceiling sounded distorted and rather eerily similar to something the hunchback of Notre Dame might've selected for his Walkman.

'Smells like a zoo in here,' said Ratso.

'That's what it is, Sergeant.'

We came to a cage with a lone elephant. As Ratso walked up to it, the animal gave forth with a loud fart, apparently signaling its displeasure.

'You've made a friend for life, Ratso.'

'I have that effect on people.'

I had stopped downwind from the elephant and was lighting a cigar when I first heard the laughter. It was tone-less and void of joy and it came cascading out of the gloom with the chill and suddenness of a Texas blue northern. It was the kind of unearthly, almost unspeakably evil sound that caused ice to begin forming along your spine.

'My God,' said Ratso. 'That better be a fucking hyena.'

'It is,' I said. 'But I'm afraid it's of the two-legged variety.'

When you're frozen in your tracks, one of the easiest things to do is listen. We listened.

The next two sounds we heard, if it is at all conceivable, rattled our cages even more.

The first was the roar of a lion.

The second was the scream of a woman.

69

'Damn everything but the circus' was the way e. e. cummings had once put it. Now, as Ratso and I dashed into the gloom, I was more than ready to throw the circus into the pot with everything else.

The only thing I wasn't ready for was the tableau of horror that lay in a pool of sick, yellow light at the end of the hall. Jane Meara's body was lying on the floor of a cage and the biggest lion I'd ever seen in my life was turning her over with a bloody claw.

I approached at a run and grasped the door of the cage. The lion tracked my movements with ancient, ruthless, sto-rybook eyes. It was staring right at me and licking its chops.

The cage itself was a fairly small enclosure – about the size of your average apartment in the Village – only it probably didn't cost fifteen hundred dollars a month. What-ever it cost, it was going to be a bitch to collect the rent.

I looked around frantically for something to put between

me and two thousand pounds of biblical hate. I found a metal folding chair.

When you know you'll soon meet a lion in person with no bars between you, a lion's eyes can tell you things about yourself that you might not pick up in a philosophy course at the university. How different in some ways, and yet how similar these eyes were to another pair of primeval orbs I'd recently encountered – the Jaguar's. One pair at least had the physiognomy of a human being, while the other belonged to a beast of the jungle. And yet both had a flat, glinting, mesmerizing quality. Of the two, it was Leo's eyes that held more compassion, more humanity. Made you think twice about the theory of evolution.

But there wasn't time to think even once. The lion roared. A soft moan came from Jane Meara's body.

It was ironic, I thought, I wasn't even a Christian.

I opened the door.

The lion stood its ground and there was something in its eyes akin to the cool, unwavering gaze of a hooker sizing up a potential john on the street. For my part, I thought of Earl Buckelew, the famous water witcher of the Texas hill country, knocking down a hornets' nest with a straw cowboy hat. I thought of Tchaikovsky or Stokowski or whatever the hell his name was, who used to walk onto the conductor's podium oblivious to the world. They say that if a brick wall had been erected across the stage, he could've walked right through it.

Whether it was a hornets' nest, an audience, or a lion, you had to use Judy Garland's little trick – pretend it wasn't there. Shake it off completely. Play only for the silent witness.

The lion roared and I damn near dropped the chair. I was edging a little closer to Jane when the beast suddenly came at me with a jungle version of a left hook. I twisted my

169

body sharply but I still caught some of it and my right arm went completely numb. I watched the metal chair go crashing against the bars. I watched the bright red blood splattering against the concrete floor. I didn't feel too much like Judy Garland and this didn't look a hell of a lot like Kansas.

Suddenly, the lion's attention seemed to be drawn to the far side of the cage. I looked over its shoulder and saw what appeared to be a human jack-in-the-box jumping up and down. It was Ratso.

Incredibly, he was getting results. Even the lion appeared to be amazed to see somebody hopping up and down like a piston, waving a coonskin cap between the bars, and shouting.

'Yo! Yo! Raw meat! Check it out!'

The lion leaped for the side of the cage, viciously swiping at the hat. I grabbed Jane with my good arm and dragged her to the door of the cage. I let go of her and awkwardly struggled to open the door, praying that Leo's attention span would stretch for a few more seconds.

It did. I got Jane out of the cage and closed the door behind us.

Ratso was down, my arm was beginning to throb, and Leo was sitting in the middle of the cage chewing peacefully on the coonskin cap.

'Everything's going to be all right,' I said to Jane.

Her eyes fluttered open and I watched them turn into mirrors of horror. I looked over my shoulder and saw it coming out of the shadows toward us.

It was another big cat, but this one walked on two feet and was carrying a gun.

70

'She wouldn't even read it! She wouldn't even look at it!'

The voice seemed to echo dully in the room like a horrifying, atonal sob. The figure moved closer and into the light, trapping Jane and myself between the gun and the cage. The gun, which we couldn't get away from. The cage, which we weren't about to go back into.

In the unhealthy, yellow light the garish cat mask looked like it came from a steam locker in some forgotten corner of hell. The gun, as near as I could tell, was not a tranquillizer gun this time. It looked a little like Rambam's revolver, only smaller. But when a gun is pointed at you, the most important thing to be aware of is that a gun is pointed at you. The size and make and model can be established later. If there is a later.

'Back in the cage! Both of you!' the creature screamed.

'No,' Jane said. Her voice sounded like that of a small tired child who'd suddenly realized it was past her lifetime.

'Yessssss,' hissed the voice, like an obscure Hindu demon.

Suddenly, the mask was off and flying against the bars of the cage. The face that was revealed looked familiar yet unfamiliar. Like someone you always thought you knew but never did. It was cold, pale, twitching, and terrible. Almost like a mask under a mask.

'Eugene!' said Jane with a sharp intake of breath.

'Who'd you expect?' he said in a low, gravelly voice. 'Robert Ludlum? Stephen King?' I couldn't be sure but it seemed as if he was frothing a bit at the mouth.

'Looks like the cat's out of the bag,' I said.

Eugene smiled. Right then he looked like the meanest son of a bitch who ever put on shoelaces.

'None of you helped me!' he shouted. 'You stood in my

way with all your little cats! Now look what's happened to you!'

He pointed the gun straight at my head.

'Eugene,' I said. 'Eugene. . .' He paused. '. . . Kinky,' he added. I could see the muscles in his face tighten at the same time his hand tightened around the trigger.

You never know what's going to happen in life. You could pick up a newspaper and see where Lady Bird Johnson was caught swimming naked in the pool at the Holiday Inn. That's what keeps us all in the game.

Jane and I held our breath.

A shot rang out.

Eugene spun around in an awkward little last waltz and hit the sawdust.

In the shadows I saw Sergeant Cooperman slowly rising out of a crouch. He and Fox walked over to us.

'Nice show,' said Sergeant Fox.

Jane, Ratso, and I were taken by ambulance to the same hospital. Ratso was fine. In fact, as he told the doctor, he'd just gone along for the ride. Jane was kept overnight for observation, and by the time I called in the morning she'd already been released. They treated my arm, said it was a flesh wound, gave me a few shots and a few prescriptions, and Ratso and I went home.

Eugene had not been as fortunate. He'd taken a ride in the stiffmobile to a nice refrigerated drawer.

Ratso never got his hat back and, quite uncharacteristically, he never even asked about it.

71

My attitude about life is you should always take the good with the bad. The game, of course, is to see if you can tell which is which.

It was Sunday night, two days after our little trip to the circus, and Ratso was packing.

'Seems like I've lived here a long time, doesn't it, Daniel?' said Ratso. Daniel was what Ratso had taken to calling me in the days immediately following my brief excursion into the lion's den. The name wasn't that humorous, but it was shorter than Nebuchadnezzar.

'Maybe Alex Haley will do a story about your stay here,' I said.

I was sitting at the desk smoking an eleven-dollar Cuban cigar I'd once bought in Vancouver. I'd been saving it for a special occasion and this was it. Getting rid of a house pest. The cat watched dispassionately from the kitchen table as Ratso packed his things. She wasn't going to believe it until she actually saw him leave.

'Uh, Daniel,' said Ratso, 'I can accept the idea of a spiritual hunch about Eugene and the circus, but run it by me one more time just how and when you began to suspect him.'

'I told you, Ratso, the pattern was there all the time. Slick Goldberg, Estelle Beekman, and Jane Meara all had in common that they were literary types. They were in one way or another involved in the publishing business.

'Eugene said something rather strange when he told Jane she should forget Rocky and get a dog. A more normal, if still somewhat insensitive, suggestion would have been to get another cat.

'After Estelle Beekman got aced, I was convinced the killer lay somewhere within the literary community with which we were dealing. Then, when Eugene told me he'd written a novel that he was having trouble getting published, he really tipped his hand. I asked him in the coffee shop that morning what the novel was about. He sidestepped the question and went into some monologue about "if Hemingway were around today he'd probably be writing ad copy."

'Now I ask you, Ratso, from what you know about human nature, have you ever heard of a novelist – especially an *unpublished* novelist – who, when asked what his book is about, declines to tell you? There ain't no such animal. It's almost clinical recall with these people.'

'So you knew,' said Ratso, 'that there was something strange about Eugene.'

'Either something strange about Eugene,' I said, 'or something about that particular manuscript that he didn't want me to know. So I had Lobster find out if he'd ever been a client of Goldberg's. He had, and Goldberg had dropped him. Also, he'd submitted the manuscript to Estelle Beekman, who'd rejected it. Meanwhile, here is Jane talking endlessly in the office about her cat, and taking forever to even read the thing. Then I find out from Landis that Eugene's book is about *dogs*. A major opus – "the *Jonathan Livingston Seagull* of dog books," Landis called it – that conceivably might've taken Eugene years to write.

'When I heard that, it absolutely tore it. A book on dogs.'

'Amazing,' said Ratso, shaking his head as he packed up his hockey equipment. 'I guess that means a foul wind is blowing for the future of my horse book.'

'Sorry about that,' I said.

I got up and walked over to the kitchen, poured out a shot of Jameson into the bull's horn, and killed the shot. I paced back and forth in the kitchen, leaving a rich trail of pre-Castro smoke in my path.

'But aside from all of this,' I said, 'what really nailed

Eugene had nothing to do with human logic or human perception at all. It was an inversion of Sherlock Holmes's famous case of the dog that didn't bark. Our case features a cat that *did* take action.'

'Rocky?' Ratso asked.

'Not Rocky, my dear Ratso, but this very cuddly little creature' – here I picked the cat off the kitchen table and briefly held it in my arms before it twisted away and tried to claw me on its way to the floor – 'this cuddly wuddly little . . .'

'Spare me,' said Ratso.

'. . . creature who once jumped on your balls. Remember?'

'It's emblazoned on my scrotum forever.'

'Well, the cat was telling you something. When the cat took a Nixon in your red antique dead man's shoe, it was also telling you something. Now you're packing up and leaving and the cat is happy.'

'So am I,' said Ratso.

'Well, I'm sure in her own way the cat will miss you.'

'Fuck the cat,' said Ratso.

'It hasn't got that bad yet. Now, as I was saying, there are some things that men still don't and probably never will understand about animals. For instance, beavers. Beavers build underground exits in their dams in later summer and early autumn and they seem to know just how thick the ice will be long before the winter ever comes. It's amazing, if you think about it. I saw it on *Mutual of Omaha's Wild Kingdom*.'

'That's what I tried to tell my ex-girlfriend,' said Ratso. 'Man still doesn't know a lot about beavers.'

'Humourous, if somewhat crude,' I said. I walked back over to the desk and sat down again. The cigar was killer bee.

'Now, if you will, my dear Ratso, cast your mind back to

last Thursday night, the little get-together that, in your words, was "a washout, Mr Wolfe." That night was no washout, though at the time I let it be seen as one. Actually, it was a great, if somewhat accidental, triumph. One that I had nothing to do with, but was able, at least, to observe. Fortunately, seeing was believing.'

'What the hell are you talking about?'

'I'm telling you the cat went right to the murderer. It jumped in his lap several times; it pestered him; it wouldn't leave him alone. Any cat owner will tell you how perverse cats can be. Quite often, they won't come to people who like them. They seem somehow to know just who of all your guests might have asthma, or be allergic, or be afraid, or be uptight. Thursday night was like a living lie detector test, and Eugene, fortunately for us, failed. There was something about him that we couldn't see, that was strange, evil, not right. I've seen the gentlest animals in the world become very upset around people who aren't quite right in their heads.

'Animal behavior, Ratso – very important. Not only can animals predict earthquakes and natural disasters, but sometimes they can unmask the cold, cruel mind of the killer among us.'

I took a rather languid puff on the cigar and watched the smoke drift upward toward the lesbian dance class.

'Now, where,' I asked, 'is the perla yi-yo?'

72

If you've ever emptied a tray of cat litter, you know that you hold the tray at arm's length and turn your head away as you dump the contents into the trash can. It was in this manner that I had managed to throw out possibly a quarter

176

of a million dollars' worth of perla yi-yo sometime earlier that weekend.

'Easy come, easy go,' Ratso said, after I'd returned from checking the trash Dumpster on Vandam Street. It was empty as the sky in California.

I wanted to kill Ratso. I wanted to kill the garbage men.

'Look at it this way,' Ratso said. 'You're probably the only guy in New York who's bitching about prompt, efficient garbage collection.'

I killed off the bottle of Jameson mouth to mouth, lit a fresh cigar, and walked over to the window.

'And now it would appear,' I said, 'that I'm about to lose a house pest.'

'Don't worry,' Ratso said. 'I haven't left yet.'

73

It had been raining cats and dogs all evening. One of them must've literally fallen from the sky because on this night, at the windy tail end of March, Jane Meara provided me with the other bookend to the story.

I had stocked up on liquor and tuna and I was just kind of sitting around, not quite feeling sorry for myself, when the phones rang. I went for the blower on the left. It was Jane.

'I told you never to call me at home,' I said.

'You won't believe it!' she said.

'You finished reading Eugene's manuscript?'

'Stop it, Kinky. I went to a hockey game tonight at Madison Square Garden with a friend . . .'

I sat back and listened as Jane told me her story. When she'd finished, and I'd cradled the blower, I put my feet up on the desk and smiled to myself. All I remember thinking was, I wish I had another Cuban cigar.

'But it wasn't really Rocky?' Ratso asked, as we stood close in the bar in the Monkey's Paw. It'd been about an hour since Jane's call and Ratso and I had already had a few rounds.

'All I know,' I said, 'is that it followed her from the Garden for five blocks with a glint of triumph in its eyes. Then, when Jane got to her car – '

'Brahms shot it with a bow and arrow.'

'No, Ratso. It jumped in the car with Jane. She took it home, went to work on it with soap, water, and a washcloth, and guess what?'

'What?'

'Four little white sweat socks.'

'Jesus Christ,' said Ratso. 'It's enough to make you believe there's a God.'

'Not necessarily,' I said. 'There are many things in nature that we don't understand. There's an old dead tree on our ranch in Texas that my dad won't let anybody chop down because the hummingbirds live there. My mother always used to love the hummingbirds. Every year, right around March fifteenth, you can see them start to arrive. They fly all the way from South America to that same old dead tree where they were born.'

'Well, that proves there's a God.'

'No, it doesn't.'

'What does it prove then?'

'It proves, my dear Ratso,' I said, 'that there is a hummingbird.'

Later that night, back at the loft, I was having a quiet conversation with the cat. The place looked oddly empty without Ratso's belongings strewn all over the couch.

I was sitting at my desk when I got the call from Sergeant Cooperman.

'Tex,' he said, 'I don't know how close you were to that Palestinian broad. You remember the one?'

'Yeah,' I said.

'She got whacked by one of the Jaguar's boys. Happened sometime earlier this week, we think. She left a package, though, and it's got your name on it. We went through it, of course. But I'll send a car over with it now, if that's all right.'

'Thanks,' I said.

'Sorry, Tex.'

I put down the blower very slowly. There wasn't really any hurry now. It was like being on spiritual hold without even being on the telephone. I waited.

In time, a squad car pulled up in front, a uniform got out, and I went down and got the package. I brought it back upstairs and opened it on the desk.

It was Leila's kaffiyeh.

I put the kaffiyeh around my shoulders. It was a little cold in the room. I walked over to the kitchen window and stood there for a long time. The cat came by and jumped up on the windowsill. Everything was quiet on the street. Maybe the garbage trucks were observing a moment of silence.

Together, the cat and I watched the world. I pulled the kaffiyeh a little tighter around me and gently stroked the cat. Sort of a sad, scythelike Pakistani moon was falling in the east over the warehouses.

'Next year in Jerusalem,' I said.

I was folding the kaffiyeh and putting it in the desk drawer when Ratso came barging into the loft with a copy of the *Daily News*.

'Jesus Christ,' he said, 'look at this.' He put the newspaper down on the desk and pointed to an article. The headline read: MCGOVERN NOMINATED FOR PULITZER PRIZE.

'I don't believe it,' said Ratso. 'It's for his series about you and the cocaine cartels.'

'McGovern's got talent,' I said with some little satisfaction, 'among other, rather more tedious qualities.'

'Yeah,' said Ratso, 'but a *Pulitzer*?'

'Maybe there *is* a hummingbird,' I said.

A short while later, Ratso was pillaging an order, on my tab, from the Carnegie Delicatessen, and watching some obscure sporting event on television. I was sitting at the kitchen table with a bottle of Jameson, the bull's horn, a tube of epoxy glue, and some black paint.

I was repairing the puppet head.

It was very satisfying, almost meditative sort of work. Repairing a little black puppet head when you couldn't repair your own.

Maybe the problem was that now I was between cases. Or maybe the problem was, as Sherlock himself had said, 'I have never loved.' But that wasn't really true for me. I had loved. I could've loved. It just didn't look like it was going to come my way again. Not everybody finds their Rocky in life, I thought. Some of us just find the courage to face the world alone.

The phones rang.

'I'm not here,' I said. Actually, it wasn't too far from the truth. In the background, I heard Ratso talking to someone on the blower.

'You're kiddin',' he said. 'What took you so long?' I kept working on the puppet head.

'I don't believe it,' he said. 'Jesus.' I kept working on the puppet head.

'Kinkstah!' he shouted. 'It's for you.'

'Who is it?' I asked.

'It's the girl in the peach-coloured dress,' he said.

I stared intently at the puppet head on the table.

'What the hell's going on?' shouted Ratso. 'Aren't you gonna talk to her?'

I turned the puppet head a little to one side and then a little to the other. You couldn't even tell it had been wounded.

'I'll speak to her,' I said, 'when the glue is dry.'